I0587682

By LEE OHLSON

A Shadow Comes Darkly
Ashford Hall
Faux for the Holidays

Published by DREAMSPINNER PRESS
www.dreamspinnerpress.com

Faux for the Holidays

Lee Ohlson

Published by
DREAMSPINNER PRESS

8219 Woodville Hwy #1245
Woodville, FL 32362 USA
www.dreamspinnerpress.com

This is a work of fiction. Names, characters, places, and incidents either are the product of author imagination or are used fictitiously, and any resemblance to actual persons, living or dead, business establishments, events, or locales is entirely coincidental.

Faux for the Holidays
© 2025 Lee Ohlson

2025 L.C. Chase
http://www.lcchase.com
Cover content is for illustrative purposes only and any person depicted on the cover is a model.

All rights reserved. This book is licensed to the original purchaser only. Duplication or distribution via any means is illegal and a violation of international copyright law, subject to criminal prosecution and upon conviction, fines, and/or imprisonment. Any eBook format cannot be legally loaned or given to others. No part of this book may be reproduced or transmitted in any form or by any means, electronic or mechanical, including photocopying, recording, or by any information storage and retrieval system, without the written permission of the Publisher, except where permitted by law. To request permission and all other inquiries, contact Dreamspinner Press, 8219 Woodville Hwy #1245, Woodville FL 32362 USA, or www.dreamspinnerpress.com.

Any unauthorized use of this publication to train generative artificial intelligence (AI) is expressly prohibited.

Trade Paperback ISBN: 9781641088800
Digital ISBN: 9781641088794
Trade Paperback published November 2025
v. 1.0

Chapter One

RORY WHITEHEAD was the unluckiest bastard who'd ever existed.

Okay, yes, there was that guy who'd been struck by lightning thirty times or whatever, but Rory was pretty sure that getting repeatedly smote by God wasn't a prerequisite for the man getting a promotion at work. This, however? Rory returning to Evergreen Hill, the town he'd run from as an eighteen-year-old, solely because he was trying to make partner at his firm? That was the lightning strike times thirty, the return of a prodigal son who did not want to be prodigal.

He couldn't even really complain, either, because Malcolm DuPont was the only person with him on this trip, and the thought of complaining to that man was honestly worse than getting struck by lightning. They had barely said three words to one another since leaving the city, and Rory wasn't going to break the silence now by airing his entire past to a guy he hated. He could just imagine Malcolm's reaction to the knowledge that Rory was from a small town known only for its Christmas tree farms. Some smug remark about how he'd been raised in Paris or Rome or London, whichever had given him his obnoxious accent. Further commentary on how he'd attended only the finest private schools, so he really couldn't fathom being raised in such a quaint location. Whatever he said would only hammer home his superiority to Rory, and he really wasn't in the mood for it.

Rory had left Evergreen Hill nearly nineteen years ago. The odds of running into someone who equated him with that scrawny, scared teenager were low. Rory Whitehead, fully licensed architect, confident and handsome, was not Rory Whitehead, crying on the bus out of Evergreen Hill, Vermont. Bringing up his past to Malcolm was just going to give the man fodder to get the partnership over him, and since he *knew* they'd been sent on this assignment solely for the firm to weed out which one was a better fit, he wasn't risking that.

The town sign for Evergreen Hill—Santa's Second Home!—passed by on the left, and Rory looked at it, gaze flitting over Malcolm briefly as a result. Of all the people on the planet, he'd never met someone he liked as little as Malcolm DuPont. The guy was a little taller than him, six foot four or something, and preternaturally pale, hair ash blonde and eyes a deep, disarming gray. Slim and well-dressed, Malcolm always gave off a slightly vampiric air, and his whole smug silence act only made him more intolerable. Even for the drive he was dressed in designer clothes, his black turtleneck the sort of quality that Rory could only dream about, his jeans some brand name that Rory could barely pronounce.

He loathed the guy.

"What's the street address of the lodge?" Malcolm asked, looking over at Rory, and Rory *knew* he'd only asked so he could catch Rory looking at him. Jackass.

"You can see it from here," Rory said, looking out the windshield at the Green Mountains looming just ahead, rolling green with white caps. A thrill went through him, a tug right in the pit of his stomach. As much distance as he'd put between himself and Evergreen Hill since he'd been a teenager, he'd always felt the slightest bit homesick for the mountains. Seeing them sprawling in front of the car only intensified that dormant urge. He scanned the foothills and pointed to a massive building that sat on the outskirts of town, turrets poking above the trees. "There."

"It looks like a castle," Malcolm said, and Rory bit down the impulse to tell him that when he'd been growing up, that was what they'd called it. Instead, he just hummed in agreement and settled back in his seat, watching as the houses began to grow closer together, passing from the farmland and forests on the outskirts to the clusters of stores and the Christmas market. The town was unchanged except for the fact that there were a couple of chains scattered among the local boutiques: a Starbucks had replaced one of the homey mom-and-pop cafes that had stood there for decades, and a McDonald's crowded in where Rory was pretty sure there had once been a florist.

They passed the center of town and began down the winding road that led to the lodge, Rory's nerves more on edge than he thought they would be. This close to Christmas was basically a guarantee that the lodge would have their seasonal staff in place, and the thought of one of those staff members being someone Rory knew from the old days was making his palms sweat. He rubbed them against his jeans, feeling Malcolm look at him out of the corner of his eye and ignoring him as best he could.

Evergreen trees rolled down, away from the road toward the valleys that made up the land around the town, winter already permeating the woods. Every so often the trees parted just enough for Rory to catch sight of some little stone farmhouse set back off the road, all decorated for the season, and while city-Rory would be apathetic to the idea of decorating for Christmas, country-Rory was simultaneously charmed and kind of sad. He'd known most of the people who lived in these houses, and he wondered if they were still living there or if, like him, they'd made a run out of town at the first opportunity.

The road opened up as they approached the lodge, and Rory turned his attention away from the sides of the road to the building. He and Malcolm were there to convince the owner to sell, to sketch a blueprint of the building and develop a possible renovation strategy going forward. Their architectural firm had recently gotten into the ski resort business and was looking to expand, and a place like Evergreen Hill was the perfect target. The Evergreen Lodge was well-established and popular, and according to research, the owner was the perfect demographic to sell: a family man with a great incentive to take an early retirement. It was just up to Rory and Malcolm to make that happen, since the owner had been entirely resistant to giving it up at all in preliminary talks.

It was a truly beautiful building, all stone and wood, and it towered over the surrounding forest like something out of a fairy tale. As a teenager, Rory had always worked the annual Christmas party in the ballroom of the hotel, but those days were long gone. Even before he'd been an architect, he'd found the lodge a thing of beauty, a wonder of construction from the Victorian era that had no doubt sparked his adoration for old buildings. Malcolm pulled into the rounded drive and stopped under the overhang, then looked over at Rory. "Go get checked in, and I'll park and bring the luggage," he said. "It doesn't take both of us to navigate the parking."

Rory rolled his eyes and got out of the car with his sketching bag, Malcolm driving off almost before he had the door closed. "Asshole," he mumbled, turning toward the lodge. He knew Malcolm had kicked him out so he could go smoke a cigarette in the parking lot. For some reason the guy was terrified that being caught smoking would ruin his image, but if Rory was *just* considering the aesthetics of Malcolm, he had to admit that the sight of him in his well-tailored clothes, those elegant fingers holding a cigarette, would be genuine eye candy.

That thought was not welcome, though, so he quickly shoved it aside and headed into the lodge. The entrance hall was as grand as ever, soaring ceilings and a Christmas tree easily eighteen feet tall already inside, although it hadn't been decorated yet. Rory stood there for a few moments looking at it, wondering if they'd gotten it from Craig's Tree Farm just down the road, before someone addressed him from behind. "It's beautiful, huh?"

Rory turned to find that a teenager in the lodge uniform—flannel and jeans—had approached, looking up at the tree with a sparkle in his eyes. He was struck by a pang of recognition, although he couldn't place it, not really. The boy had auburn hair that curled slightly on top, his eyes hazel and gleaming with a striking intelligence. He was still freckled despite the summer being long gone, and when Rory looked at him the kid smiled, lopsided and a little goofy. "We really lucked out this year. I can't remember having a tree this big since I was a kid. Although… I was a kid, so maybe they just always seemed bigger than they actually were."

"Did you get it from Craig's?" Rory asked, and the kid's grin grew.

"You know Craig? Yeah, although he was giving my dad a lot of pushback on picking out this one. He was trying to convince the city to take it for the Christmas market. Dad wore him down, though."

"Your dad owns the lodge?"

"Yep!" The kid stuck out his hand, and Rory shook it, surprised to find the teen had a firmer grip than he'd been anticipating. "Jasper Daniels."

"Rory Whitehead," Rory said, before recognition lurched through him like being hit by a Mack truck.

A calloused hand in his own, tugging him excitedly through the avenues between the trees on the back forty behind the Daniels's farmhouse, in the family for centuries. A mouth against his, warm and familiar, in the back of the truck Samuel had bought with his first paycheck when he was sixteen. Auburn curls, hazel eyes, freckled skin. Jasper was a clone of his father, the only man Rory had ever actually loved, and the realization that he was standing face-to-face with the offspring of Samuel fucking Daniels made his stomach seize up, his anxiety proving well-founded.

Jasper was giving him a weird look too. "Sorry, you said your name is Rory Whitehead?" He glanced over his shoulder toward the door that Rory knew led back to the kitchen of the lodge, frowning. "Wait here." With that, he took off at a breakneck pace, shoving through the kitchen door. He was back there for less than ten seconds before he came bursting out again, seeming to check that Rory was still there before giving him a thumbs-up.

The thumbs-up made Rory even more frightened than before. If Samuel came out of those kitchen doors, there was a 98 percent chance Rory was going to faint right then and there. The double door pushed open, and there he was, almost twenty years older and handsome in a way that made Rory's heart hurt. Worst of all, Rory saw those hazel eyes light up and *knew* that as badly as he'd missed Samuel since leaving Evergreen Hill, Samuel had missed him too.

"Rory?" he said, disbelief dripping from his voice as he wiped his hands on a towel, approaching him slowly. He was wearing a green flannel with a khaki-colored apron over top, flour dusted across the front, and although they were nearly forty, his hair was untouched by gray, his age indicated mostly by the endearing crow's feet at the corners of his eyes and the auburn stubble across his jaw. "I thought Jasper was lying."

"Why would I lie about something like that?" Jasper asked, grabbing the towel from his father and pushing his dad toward Rory.

Samuel approached warily, as though he was worried Rory was a mirage that would disappear if he got too close. Rory stared at him, eyes inadvertently flitting toward Samuel's left hand and spotting the wedding ring there. Heart beating out of his chest, he nevertheless managed a smile. "You own the lodge? You always did love this place."

"I didn't see you on the guest list," Samuel said.

"Oh, I'm booked under the Keye-Larson Architecture firm," Rory said, putting his hands in his cardigan pockets to disguise how sweaty he'd gotten and to avoid having to shake Samuel's hand. The thought of touching him after so many years apart made his stomach hurt.

"You're an architect!" Jasper said, having come up behind his dad. "That's crazy. Dad always hoped—"

"Jas," Samuel said, grinning at his son, and the moment he did the family resemblance became even clearer. "Go pull up the room for Rory and get him the key, okay?"

"Got it," Jasper said, darting over to the desk, and Rory was hit by a memory of Samuel, running full speed because Rory had mentioned that the smell of cinnamon rolls wafting from the town bakery was driving him crazy. Samuel smiled at him, clearly taking the hint and not offering Rory his hand to shake.

"You're thinking about how much I used to run like that, aren't you?"

"No, of course not," Rory said, laughing. "Although to be honest, I think he *might* be faster than you. I guess my job isn't a surprise?"

"Rory, every bit of you being here is a surprise," Samuel said, brow furrowing. "It's eight days before Christmas, and I haven't seen you in twenty years. You're really here on a work thing?"

"Yeah," Rory said. "My firm wants to see what kind of business goes on during the holiday season, so…. Here I am."

"You *really* didn't know I'd bought the place?"

"I really didn't know," Rory said. "I swear." He left off the part where he wouldn't have come if he'd known the place was owned by Samuel. Seeing him was impossibly painful, as if someone was scraping their nails over freshly burned skin, and all he wanted to do was go upstairs and wallow in it, although with Malcolm here he couldn't exactly do that.

"What's going on here?" As if on cue, Malcolm walked up behind him, pulling both suitcases and smelling like peppermint gum, a sure sign he'd been smoking. It was infuriating, humiliating, and Rory couldn't stop thinking about that ring on Samuel's finger and the teenager behind the desk. "Is there trouble with the room?"

Samuel's gaze flitted to Malcolm, and Rory saw it, saw the flicker of confusion in his eyes and then the flicker of something that looked a hell of a lot like jealousy. That look, more than anything else, was the only reason Rory had for what he did next. "Who's this?" Samuel asked, plastering on a polite smile, and before Malcolm could say anything Rory's hand shot back, gripping Malcolm's forearm as hard as he could.

"This is Malcolm DuPont, my coworker and fiancé." He squeezed Malcolm's arm and forced a smile. "Malcolm, this is Samuel Daniels. We grew up together."

He looked up at Malcolm, who had no expression on his face whatsoever, and blinked in surprise as Malcolm stuck his hand out to Samuel. "Pleased to meet you."

Samuel shook his hand in return but dropped his hand back to his side almost immediately after, glancing over at the front desk, where Jasper was at the computer. "I'm sorry, if I'd known you were together, I'd have given you a room with a single bed," he said. "I gave you one with two queens."

"That's fine," Malcolm said. "We don't need much space when we're sleeping." There was a tone in his voice that Rory wasn't used to, an almost mischievous slant, and he shot him a look that Malcolm did not return.

"What's your accent?" Samuel asked. "We get a lot of international travelers, but yours is quite unique."

"Scotland," Malcolm said, pale eyes darting to Jasper as the kid finally returned, holding a pamphlet and a pair of room keys. "Is this your son?"

Samuel nodded, gripping Jasper by the back of the neck and smiling. "Yep. Spitting image, huh?"

"Absolutely," Malcolm said. "Is he trained to work the front desk?"

Samuel's smile faded. "Yes."

"Then why did it take him so long?" Malcolm asked, holding out his hand for the keys. "Maybe he should be retrained."

"Noted," Samuel said, giving Rory a stunned look before stepping back. "It was nice to see you, Rory. I'm glad you're here for Christmas." Without waiting for a response, he turned on his heel and walked back to the kitchen, letting the doors slam behind him.

Jasper watched his father go before turning his attention back to Rory, giving him a small and embarrassed smile. "It was nice to finally meet you," he said quietly. "If you need anything while you're staying here, call the front desk. One of us will answer."

"Got it," Rory said, regretting everything he'd done in the past five minutes. He looked at Malcolm, who was pointedly *not* looking at him, and grabbed his suitcase. "Let's go."

The walk to the stairs was a quiet one, much like their entire car ride up here, and it wasn't until they were in their room that Malcolm said anything at all. "So," he said, settling on the bed nearest the door and looking at Rory. "Would you like to explain just what is going on?"

Chapter Two

JASPER WATCHED Rory walk up the double stairs that led to the second story of the lodge, glancing over his shoulder briefly at the kitchen door where his father had disappeared. He knew his dad better than anything on the planet, and the wall of ice that had dropped between him and Rory as soon as the fiancé had come on the scene was impossible to ignore. As badly as he wanted to follow his dad back to the kitchen, though, he had to watch the front desk. He wasn't going to give the asshole with the accent a reason to complain about him more.

He returned to the front desk, sighing and watching the entrance hall. Honestly, they were in their pre-Christmas lull, most families only coming for the few days before the holiday and after. Aside from the architects, there was only one other reservation on the books for the night, and they had called to say that their flight from Paris wasn't landing until later that evening. The chance of some other guests coming in was slim, but not none.

It didn't track. Rory Whitehead, punk kid who'd had the guts to leave Evergreen Hill and follow his dreams, had haunted his father's life since before Jasper had been born. They had pictures of him in their photo albums, faded Polaroid selfies of the pair of them. Rory, dark-skinned and handsome, brown eyes crinkling at the corners as he grinned at the camera, and his dad…. Eyes never on the lens, always focused on Rory like he was ten times more interesting than whatever they were trying to document.

Then there was *the* Polaroid, the one Jasper had found stuck to the back of a picture of Rory and his dad in the bed of Samuel's pickup truck. Jasper had heard the story a hundred times, how his dad had worked his ass off at a Christmas tree farm saving for the truck, but as the adhesive in the album had worn down, the corner of another picture had become visible. That picture, the one that had simultaneously flipped Jasper's world upside down and put every last piece of the puzzle into place.

Jasper glanced at the kitchen door to make sure his dad wasn't on his way back out and reached under the desk for his backpack, hauled it out and dug through it to find his sketchbook. He flipped through it to the back, the stolen Polaroid there among his hasty pencil sketches of guests, and his heart gave a little flip. It was committed to memory by this point, but seeing it only reinforced Jasper's gut feeling that something had gone terribly wrong today. It was the only solid evidence he had that Rory and his dad had once been in love—genuine romantic love, not anything platonic.

They had to be his age, eighteen or a little bit older, and the picture had been taken at the exact moment when they'd kissed. His dad was still half smiling, his mouth pressed against Rory's. Rory had his hand up, fingers tangled lightly in his dad's auburn hair, eyes closed as he leaned into the kiss. Frozen in time, tangible proof of what they'd meant to one another. Jasper had always wanted to meet Rory, but now that he had, everything felt wrong.

"Jas."

Jasper lifted his head, shoving the Polaroid back into his sketchbook as his dad came back out from the kitchen. "What's up?"

"I'm sorry about that," Samuel said, glancing toward the stairs. "I lost my temper."

Jasper frowned, turning so his back was against the front desk and pushing himself up so he was sitting on it. He'd shot up quite a bit over the last year and was nearly as tall as his dad, but it was nice to have just that little bit of extra height. "Dad, come on. I'm not blind."

Samuel frowned back at him, although Jasper could tell that he was just being mocked. "Then why did I have to spend a fortune on contacts for you?"

Jasper rolled his eyes. "That's good. Really. How long have you been thinking of that?"

"Came up with it on the fly," Samuel said, snapping his fingers at Jasper, and despite himself Jasper laughed. "What are you talking about, Jas?"

Jasper sighed, fiddling with the sleeve of his flannel as he flip-flopped between revealing the existence of the Polaroid to his dad and keeping it to himself. He had never intended to tell his dad that he knew about that part of him, figured there was a reason for him to raise Jasper thinking that Rory was just his long-lost best friend and not his first love, but he had also never really expected Rory to come waltzing back into their lives with a fiancé that looked like he had emerged from the pages of GQ.

He reached over to his sketchbook and opened it, removed the Polaroid and held it out to his father. Samuel took it, forehead crinkled in confusion, and the look that passed over his face confirmed what Jasper already knew: seeing Rory today had opened up some old wounds. There was softness there, regret, longing, and then he looked at Jasper again and frowned, this time for real. "Where did you get this?"

"It was in one of our photo albums, stuck behind another picture," Jasper admitted. "I've had it for a couple years now." He looked down, picking at a scar on the wooden desk. "I know I should have given it to you, but it just... it made me feel like I understood you better, I guess. Like I always knew Rory meant a lot to you, but knowing that you loved him.... It made me feel closer to you."

Samuel looked at the Polaroid, smiling despite himself. "We took this the day before he left," he said, and much to Jasper's surprise he handed the picture back to him before walking over to join him in sitting on the desk. "I never told you about this part of our relationship because I never wanted you to think that I wasn't happy with just you," Samuel said after a few long moments of silence.

Jasper looked at his dad, clearly confused. "What do those two things have to do with each other?" he asked.

"I.... You know I was so young when you came along, right?" Samuel asked, turning slightly so he was facing Jasper. "After Rory left, I was so miserable. You really helped change that, but I was planning on following him when I got the chance. Having you prevented that from happening, and I didn't...." He trailed off, tilting his head back so he could look at the ceiling instead of his son.

Jasper frowned, reaching out and covering one of his dad's hands with his own. "Dad, if you're gay, I don't care. I mean, not in a mean way. And I don't think you hold anything against me. You've always loved me more than I probably deserve sometimes. I just want you to be happy, and...." He looked at the Polaroid again, smiling. "You guys look *really* happy."

"We were. We were inseparable, basically from birth. When he left, it broke me for a really long time." He huffed out a soft laugh. "I thought I'd gotten over it, but seeing him today really threw that back in my face. He's only gotten more handsome." Samuel sighed, dragging his thumb over his lower lip. "That fiancé of his, though...."

"Jackass," Jasper agreed, making a face. "I was trying to figure out if I could upgrade their suite. That's the only reason it took that long. When you talk about Rory, it's always about what a punk he was. Why would he be with a jackass like that?"

"It's pretty likely that the Rory I knew isn't the Rory that's here," Samuel said. "Who knows what New York has done to him? Anyway, I just wanted to make sure that you knew that you didn't do anything wrong. That guy was just one rude guest, and I can't run this place without you."

"Oh, trust me, I know," Jasper said, grinning. "You don't know how to restart the Wi-Fi router."

"Okay, not true," Samuel said. "I just cut power to the whole lodge and go from there, right?" He turned to head back into the kitchen before pausing, looking back at his son briefly. "Don't—well, don't worry about me selling the lodge, either. We're doing well, and I don't want to give it up to some firm that will strip out all its independence. I've always kind of hoped you would take it over."

"Maybe when I'm sixty," Jasper said, screwing his face up in faux disgust despite knowing full well that he would gladly take over the lodge when his dad decided the time was right.

Samuel laughed as he headed back into the kitchen, waving his hand dismissively at his son over his shoulder as he went, and Jasper watched him go before sliding off the desk and looking at the Polaroid again. God, his dad looked so happy. He was going to make this right, going to ensure that Rory and his dad at least mended fences, even if they couldn't rekindle their love. They knew nothing about Rory after he'd left Evergreen Hill except that he was clearly an architect now, and Jasper figured that was as good a spot to start as any.

He'd just pulled up an article about Rory's work on designing a new civic center in Brooklyn when the front doors to the lodge opened and a man entered, dragging a suitcase behind him. Jasper looked at him before switching back to the hotel software, double-checking the reservations. As he thought, the only reservation for the night was for the Caldwells, and they were a party of three. Unless the father had been sent on ahead to check them in, this wasn't the Caldwells.

"Hi there!" Jasper said brightly nonetheless. "Welcome to Evergreen Lodge."

"Thanks," the guy said, sounding friendly but otherwise exhausted. He approached the front desk, shaking his head like a wet dog, and a few snowflakes clinging to his hat fell off. Jasper looked at the huge windows behind the Christmas tree and saw that it had started to snow, pretty heavily from the looks of it. "I'm so sorry, I know I don't have a reservation, but I was supposed to be staying in an Airbnb down in the village, and it's been double-booked. The owner wasn't sure, but she thought maybe you guys would still have a room available."

"Oh, man, that sucks," Jasper said, already pulling up the booking page. "Uh, how long are you looking to stay?"

"I'm a photographer," the guy said, still looking agitated. "I'm supposed to be here taking photos to scout a new location for a movie, and—"

"You're supposed to be here through Christmas," Jasper said, grimacing. "Got it. Okay, I'm not gonna promise you anything, but let me see what I can do. What's your name?"

"Ty Choi," the man said. Jasper typed it in, asking the man the regular questions for guests and thinking of what they could do if there wasn't a spot available. Ty looked harried, tired, but he was still handsome, almond-shaped eyes that were a deep, charming brown, and if Jasper had to guess he'd put him in his early thirties, an estimate confirmed by the date on his driver's license. "You seem kind of young to be running a hotel."

"Ah, my dad owns it," Jasper said. "I'm just the help. This is kind of the only thing he trusts me to do." He bit his lower lip, scanning the booking software. "Okay. I think we can do it, but it'll require a bit of flexibility on your end."

"I am as flexible as can be," Ty said. "What do you need me to do?"

"So right now the honeymoon suite doesn't have anyone in it," Jasper said. "It's free until the twenty-second, and then we have a wedding party coming in. I'm gonna put you there, because it's the only room that's really untouched until that time. After that, though, there aren't any hotel rooms available over Christmas."

"Shit."

"No, don't worry," Jasper said. "There's no *hotel* rooms available, but my dad and I live in what used to be the servant's quarters, and we've got plenty of empty rooms back there. Our seasonal staff are in most of them, but there's for sure a spot for you." He raised his eyebrows at Ty. "But it'll cost you."

"Oh, my company is paying for this, so—"

"I was thinking that maybe you could take updated pictures for our website in exchange for staying in the staff quarters," Jasper said, looking at Ty. "It would be a huge, huge help, man."

Ty grinned, looking at Jasper with some surprise. "Really? Just like that?"

"Just like that," Jasper said. "If you were sent up here by someone in town, then me and my dad will work to make that right. But we also really need new pictures, and I'm not that good. Is it a deal?"

"I think it's totally fair," Ty said. "Your dad's gonna agree?"

"Yeah, I can convince him," Jasper said. "Let's get you your room key, huh?"

Chapter Three

"… SO I SAW his wedding ring and didn't want to seem like the loser who was coming crawling back to his hometown, so I just… said you were my fiancé," Rory finished, pacing up and down the length of the room as Malcolm sat there and watched him, the expression on his face absolutely impossible to read. Now that they were upstairs, the panic was real, Rory's heart racing as he realized exactly what he'd done. Not only had he completely undone any chances of reconciling with Samuel, he'd also essentially shown Malcolm his entire deck of cards.

Malcolm considered him, not saying anything, and when he finally did speak, his annoyance was clear. "This is very inconvenient for me," he said.

That stopped Rory from pacing, his gaze fixated on Malcolm. "Sorry?"

"We're here on a business trip, Whitehead. A trip to figure out how easy it will be to get this man to sell us his lodge. Your high school romance and all the fallout from it is not something I want to be dealing with. It's already inconvenient enough, having to spend Christmas with you. Spending Christmas with you pretending to be your fiancé? It's an annoyance."

"Then why did you play along? That's an insane thing for you to do if you're annoyed."

"It's an insane thing for you to pretend that I'm your fiancé," Malcolm shot back, and for the first time there was a bit of bite to his words, an acid that he usually reserved for interns who got his coffee order wrong… or teenage boys who took too long to check him into a hotel. "I played along because it was the only way to salvage this trip. We can't exactly do our jobs if Samuel thinks you're a liar who's still in love with him. And if his wife is on the scene?"

His wife. Rory's stomach turned at the idea, misery flooding him in waves. Judging by the age of Jasper, it had taken Samuel a year or less to get married and knock a girl up, whatever order that had come in. In that time, Rory had been basically bedridden with misery, able to leave his dorm only to go to class and do very little else. He'd thought—maybe even hoped a little—that Samuel had been pining the same way. The fact that he hadn't, that he'd been so unaffected by Rory's departure that he'd immediately married a girl....

He sat down hard on the edge of his bed, gripping the mattress tightly. Now he felt stupid *and* childish, and he still had to spend ten days with Malcolm on top of it. "So what now?"

"There's two options," Malcolm said, leaning back on his hands and watching Rory with that cool and calm expression on his handsome face. God, Rory hated him. "First, we go downstairs and we tell Samuel the truth. That we're nowhere near engaged, that you lied to his face out of some misguided idea that it would… make him jealous? Is that close enough?"

"Not jealous," Rory said, frowning. "I didn't want him to think that I'd just been… waiting around for him all this time."

"But you have."

"No, you asshole, I haven't. I've gone on plenty of dates." After the first five years of pure misery, sure, but Malcolm didn't need to know that. "What's option two?"

"We keep lying and you withdraw from the partnership competition for the next year."

Rory's blood ran cold. "What?"

"And endorse me to the board."

"What?" Rory shook his head, his mouth dry from the shock of what Malcolm had just proposed. "I've been fighting for partner for almost ten years now. I'm not—"

"Going anywhere anytime soon, so another year won't kill you," Malcolm said, ice dripping from his words. "Think about this rationally, Whitehead. If you say no to this and we go downstairs and tell Samuel, we lose this entire deal. You'll lose the partnership anyway, and you'll drag me down with you. Might even lose your job for not disclosing your family ties to this place."

"They wouldn't fire me for that."

"You don't sound sure, and why risk it? I'm offering you a quid pro quo."

"It kind of seems like blackmail," Rory said quietly. "But… I don't want Samuel to find out I lied. Fuck, out of everyone at work, I had to come here with you, didn't I. Just my fucking luck." He pushed himself up off the bed, turned around to face the balcony, walked over, and looked out across the mountains toward the town. "If I agree to this, you swear you're not going to double-cross me?"

"I'm not interested in humiliating you to the man we're here to impress," Malcolm said, annoyed. "The truth is, I just want to do this job and do it well. If that means being forced to hold your hand, I can endure it."

Rory turned back to look at him. "But you're straight."

Malcolm smiled thinly, almost amused. "Why do you think that? Because I don't think I told you anything regarding my sexuality, considering how clearly obnoxious I find yours. Let me worry about how I feel about posing as your fiancé, aside from the obvious moral failings of it." He eyed Rory. "Now, I've driven for a long time today. I'm exhausted, and I'd like to lay down before dinner. Do you mind either getting out or staying quiet?"

God, he was rude. Rory blinked at him, flabbergasted, and then shook his head, grabbing his room key. "No. I'll go wander, take some sketches. Just checking, though…. They teach you the word 'please' in Scotland, right?"

"No, I've never heard that word before," Malcolm said dryly. "You'll need to teach me about it after I've slept. Now go. And when you get back, I want your answer." Rory didn't react, and Malcolm sighed, the corner of his lip twitching into a near-sneer. "About the partnership."

Rory frowned, running his tongue over his teeth as he tried to think of a parting shot and failed. Instead, he just headed out the door, his head down as he tried to figure out why Malcolm was so quick to get under his skin but also so quick to agree to what he had pulled him into. "Fucking weirdo," he said as he headed downstairs, finding Jasper still at the front desk. "Hey, Jasper."

Jasper looked at him, his eyes suddenly large and surprised. "Oh, uh, hi."

"Oh no," Rory said. "Don't say hi like that."

"Like what?"

"Like you wish I'd stayed up in my room." Rory walked over to the desk, looking at the teenager and feeling that same déjà vu he'd had when he'd first seen him. "Has anyone ever told you that you look exactly like your dad?"

"Yeah, I hear it all the time," Jasper said, smiling. "I promise I don't wish you'd stayed up in your room. I wanted, uh… I wanted to talk to you, actually." He looked over his shoulder at the kitchen, clearly wondering if his father was going to reappear, and Rory was absolutely prepared for the kid to ask about their relationship when Jasper looked back at him. "When you left, you went to NYU, right?"

"Oh, yeah," Rory said. "I got a scholarship or I don't think I'd have been able to go. You're at the age where you're starting to get offers, huh?"

"Yeah, I graduate in the spring," Jasper said, rubbing at the back of his neck, clearly embarrassed by what he wanted to ask. "I'm planning on taking art, but I'm…. New York seems way bigger than what I'm used to. I guess I just wanted to ask someone who'd done the same thing about it."

Rory was hit by a sudden affection for the kid, smiling despite himself. "Okay, I can answer any questions you have. I won't lie to you, though. When I left… I didn't have a support system here, so it was easier for me to leave than it will be for you."

"No support system…." Jasper considered the Polaroid, his brow furrowing, and Rory wondered how much Jasper really knew about his relationship with Samuel. "Not even my dad?"

Rory dragged his thumb over his lower lip, caught off guard by the question. "No," he said. "By then, I didn't have your dad. But that's not the point. *You've* got your dad." For the first time, he considered the fact that if Jasper left for college, it would put Samuel right back to where he'd been when Rory had left: alone. "He won't try and stop you from leaving, though."

"I know he wouldn't," Jasper said. "But I think knowing that I could come back from New York at any time and my dad would love me the same would make it easier to go."

Rory smiled, watching the teenager carefully. "That's a good way to look at it. I know how much your dad loves you."

Jasper peered at him, clearly weighing out the question he wanted to ask. "How'd you meet your fiancé?"

"Oh, Malcolm? Uh… we met at work." Not a lie, and it seemed like a normal, suitable place for a couple to meet. "He joined the firm about a year after I started."

"Was it love at first sight?" Jasper asked, and Rory laughed.

"That only exists in movies," Rory said, leaving out the part where he didn't love Malcolm in the slightest to begin with. "So you're an artist?"

"I'd like to be," Jasper said, taking out his sketchbook and opening it to a page with a small watercolor of the lodge. He pushed it over to Rory, smiling. "I'm preparing a portfolio for submission, but I always have my sketchbook with me. I like to draw guests."

"Really?" Rory asked, looking at the painting with interest. "Are you going to draw me?"

"I… well, I've already drawn you," Jasper admitted, taking the sketchbook back and flipping through it until he found a page, then setting it back down on the desk. Rory looked at it, finding his younger self looking up at him in pencil. "We have a lot of pictures of you around the house. I always thought you were really interesting to draw."

"Me?" Rory asked, laughing as he looked at the sketch. "You've made me look a lot more handsome than I actually am."

"That's not true!" Jasper grinned at him, Rory mildly surprised by how quickly the teenager had taken to him. "You looked so cool when you were a teenager. Dad's got one picture of you from when you guys went to a Green Day concert, and you're actually incredible. All ripped jeans and a Mohawk."

"Oh God, I forgot I had that," Rory said, touching his hair, which he'd let grow into natural curls once he'd gotten to New York City and realized his look wasn't really anything new in a place that big. "He had his hair dyed that summer too. It was supposed to be teal, but it turned into this horrible Windex color after he washed it a couple times, so then he pretended that he had gotten super into baseball caps all of a sudden."

"Seriously? He's never told me that story!"

"I'm sure there's plenty of stories he never told you," Rory said, grinning. "Like the time we stole his cousin's fishing boat to go out on the lake and he fell overboard and pulled me in after him. And the time—"

"If you keep telling my son about my delinquent years, I'll beat you up," Samuel said, coming out of the kitchen and setting a plate in front of Jasper. "Cinnamon rolls are done."

"You couldn't beat me up if you had a lead pipe," Rory said, waving his hand in the air to disguise how his heart had started to beat uncontrollably the second he'd seen Samuel come out. "When did you start baking?"

"Oh, Juliet's been teaching me," Samuel said, pointing to the kitchen, and Rory glanced at the doors, a dozen thoughts flitting through his mind before he landed on the most likely one, confirmed by the next words out of Samuel's mouth. "You remember Juliet Parker from school, right?"

Beautiful, confident, and just Samuel's type. Of course it was Juliet Parker he'd married. Rory nodded, hoping against hope that Samuel hadn't noticed the way his entire body had gone stiff at the mention of the woman. He had always liked her, and being confronted with his own sudden jealousy made him feel like an asshole. "Yeah, of course I remember Juliet," Rory said. "What are the cinnamon rolls for?"

"Breakfast, obviously," Samuel said. "Your company told you that all meals are covered, right?"

"Oh, I thought they told me something about that," Rory said, smiling. "It's really a little self-contained city up here, huh?"

Samuel nodded, looking at Jasper as his son began to pull the cinnamon roll apart and eat it from the outside in. "Oh, come on, Jas, eat it like a normal kid."

"No, I like to rip it up," Jasper said, mouth already full. "You should make cinnamon rolls that are just the inside part."

"That's… not possible," Samuel said, sighing and running his hand back through his hair before looking at Rory again. "Actually, I'm glad you're down here," he said. "I wanted to talk to you."

THIS WAS like watching a tennis match where one of the players was just getting repeatedly struck by the other player's racket—which might actually just be a beating? Jasper was trying not to make it too obvious that he was staring at both of the older men in turn, but his dad was acting like he was totally oblivious, and Rory looked like he was about to go screaming out into the snow, his body language so tense it was making Jasper uncomfortable in return.

"Dad," he hissed, gesturing for his father to come over to him with both hands. Samuel frowned, glancing at Rory before walking over to his son. Jasper grabbed his dad by the head, ignoring how sticky his fingers were from the cinnamon roll icing, and yanked him down, speaking in a low whisper. "What are you doing?"

"I just want to talk to him," Samuel whispered back, looking at Jasper with clear confusion. "What's the matter?"

"Isn't that inappropriate? His fiancé is right upstairs, right?"

"What do you think I'm going to do to him?" Samuel asked, raising his hands to grab his son's wrists. "Let go of my head. I'll be back in a minute."

"Everything okay?" Rory asked, peering at them both, and Jasper let go of Samuel, giving him a look that clearly told him to be on his best behavior before his dad walked back over.

"Yeah, come on," Samuel said, gesturing for Rory to follow him, and the pair of them disappeared into the kitchen, Rory keeping a fair distance behind Samuel. God, Jasper was curious. He wanted to know so badly what had gone wrong between the two men, but he didn't think either of them would tell him, and… well, no matter what his ideals about true love were, the fact remained that Rory had a fiancé upstairs, even if that fiancé was a dickhead.

"Please have a conversation in the kitchen so Juliet can tell me all the gossip later," Jasper whispered, closing his sketchbook and secreting it beneath the desk once again.

Chapter Four

RORY FOLLOWED Samuel, unable to ignore the tense slope of the other man's shoulders as they entered the kitchen. God, he'd gotten big. When he'd left for New York, Samuel had still been about his size, the pair of them pretty evenly matched in height and strength, but the years of separation had clearly done him good. He was three or four inches taller than Rory now, broader in the shoulders than Rory had ever been even when he'd been good about going to the gym, and his hair….

No wonder he'd panicked and lied when he'd seen him. It was a nightmare situation, coming face-to-face with your first love and finding that he was ridiculously handsome, happily married, and the father of a kid who clearly adored him. God, he was embarrassed. "What do you want to talk about?" he asked, and Samuel held up one hand, continuing to lead Rory deeper into the kitchen.

"Why are you bringing a guest back here?" There was a woman—Juliet, no doubt—standing at a workbench, her dark hair pulled back in a ponytail and her apron dusted with flour as she worked on some dough. Rory thought she was actually pretty familiar still, despite twenty years apart, and he clenched his jaw as he looked at her and saw the wedding ring on her finger. Christ. So he hadn't been having an overactive imagination. She had actually married Samuel.

"He's not a guest," Samuel said, and Rory could hear that tone in his voice, the one he used when he was pouting about something. It used to be so easy to roast him for it, to pry whatever had upset him right out of the vault he kept it in, but he doubted it would be easy these days. He didn't have any hold over Samuel anymore. "It's Rory."

"Rory?" Juliet asked, and her shock was evident even as Rory walked past her without looking, hoping the cloud of total inhospitality he was giving off would be enough to deter any further questions. "What are you doing here?"

"Work," Rory said, continuing to follow Samuel. "Where are we going?"

Samuel didn't respond, pushing through another pair of double doors. The winter air hit Rory like a truck, and Samuel led him out onto a side porch, well-covered from the snow but still chilly. He walked over to a bench undoubtedly set out there for that purpose and dug through his pockets, then pulled out a pack of cigarettes and a lighter as Rory watched him uncomfortably from the doorway. Samuel fumbled out a cigarette and lit it on the third try, the wind blowing in off the mountains enough to prevent it from working the first few times.

"Did you bring me out here to watch you smoke?" Rory asked, glancing over his shoulder as he stepped outside, let the doors close behind him, and wrapped his arms around himself, wishing he'd grabbed a coat but aware that he didn't really have any reason to think he'd be going outside. At least his sweater was fairly thick.

"Do you want one?" Samuel asked, looking at him, and Rory was struck by the look on his face, the corners of his eyes pinched and tired. "I don't think you smoke."

"I don't," Rory said. "I'm surprised you do."

"Rarely. Come sit down."

Rory approached the bench but didn't sit, standing next to the end and looking down at Samuel. The idea of sitting beside him, feeling the warmth coming off his body, was a punishment he probably deserved but simply couldn't stomach. He forced himself to look away, turning his attention to the mountains, the snow coming down in fat, fluffy flakes. It was his favorite kind of snow, the sort that muffled everything and made the entire world seem quiet. How many days had he and Samuel spent sitting in Samuel's basement, sharing a blanket, watching some shitty horror movie and watching the snow fall through the window?

That those days were gone now and would never return was sad in a way he simply couldn't fathom. He leaned against the side of the lodge, and Samuel looked up at him, his eyes softening slightly. "I wanted to talk to you about your fiancé," he said, steeling himself. "He can't be talking to Jasper like that." He took a drag off his cigarette, looking back out at the snow. "If it was just a rude guest, I'd let it go, but it's not. It's *you*. Why would you even be with someone like that?"

Rory wished he could have said that he wasn't, that he'd panicked, that he'd barely even had a boyfriend since he'd left Evergreen Hill because he was incapable of dating a guy without immediately comparing him to Samuel. But then he thought of Juliet in the kitchen and Jasper out at the front desk. The life that Samuel had built for himself after Rory had left was the exact life Rory would have wanted for him, and he didn't want to inject himself into it. He just had to fake it for a bit and then go home, back to a city where he no longer felt he belonged. "He can be abrupt," Rory said, sliding his hands in his jean pockets. "I'll talk to him."

Samuel frowned, ashing his cigarette before looking up at Rory, the sight of him making something hungry twist up in his gut. Maybe that hunger had never really gone away, had always just been lurking beneath the surface, and seeing Rory was just waking it back up. "How did you not know that I owned the lodge?"

"All my prep for coming here was looking up old building plans and that type of research. Malcolm is the one who researched the manpower, and since no one at the company knows where I came from, no one would have known to ask me about it."

"I don't even want to sell the lodge in the first place, Rory. If you'd done an ounce of digging on how much has changed in town since you were here, you'd have known that much." Samuel breathed out through his nose, a classic tell from their childhood that told Rory he was desperately trying to keep himself calm. "So you were just planning on coming here and not seeing me?"

Rory stared at the snow, coming thicker now, and wondered what it would feel like to just walk out into the blizzard, lie down in the snow, go to sleep. Evergreen Hill had made him feel suffocated as a teenager, and now he was feeling suffocated all over again for an entirely different reason. He'd often dreamed of the return to his hometown, everything in rose-colored tones as he reunited with Samuel, but that was just being naive. Samuel couldn't wait for him for twenty years, and Rory couldn't expect him to, not when he was the one who left. "I had no plans to come see you," Rory said, refusing to look over at Samuel. "I'm here for work."

"Jesus," Samuel breathed out, staring up at Rory. Anger flashed in his pale eyes, and Rory could read that look as easily now as he had been able to as a teenager. No doubt Samuel was wrestling with what he definitely saw as Rory's betrayal, his expression an open book, and it made that hurt part of Rory want to lash out and hurt him back. "That's fucked up."

"I guess so," Rory said quietly. "It was a conscious decision too. I decided before I even left the city that I wasn't going to seek you out. I didn't want to see you."

"Why?" Samuel asked, putting out his cigarette in the ashtray and sighing. "You really weren't curious about what was going on with me?"

"Of course I was curious," Rory said. "But I already left you once. Why would I come back here and visit you when I knew I had to leave again? Worse, why would I visit you just to see how much better your life is without me in it?"

Samuel rubbed at his forehead, another tell that he was trying to keep himself from exploding. "My life isn't better without you in it," he said. "It's just different than it would have been if you'd stayed. You're so dramatic. Guess that hasn't changed. I just thought… if it was me, I'd have done whatever I could to come and see you."

The admission sent a chill through Rory, his fingers flexing in his pockets. "I didn't want to see you, okay? You have no idea how long it took for me to get over leaving here in the first place, Sam. Years and years of just—"

"What? Wondering why I never got on that bus with you?" Samuel stood up, turning to look at Rory and crossing his arms over his chest, his face flushed from the cold. "The answer is inside manning the front desk. If you'd trusted me and waited even just one more day, I could have explained myself, but you just… left."

A chill went straight through Rory, unrelated to the weather. "Jasper?"

"His age is obviously pretty close to the time you left, isn't it?" Samuel asked, and Rory wished he'd stop looking at him like that, a mixture of anger and regret in his eyes. Rory wanted to reach out and grab him, but he was too much of a coward. That hadn't changed, either. "Do the math."

"You got a girl pregnant before I even left town?" Rory had to look away, his chest all twisted up. For years he'd assumed that Samuel had been the same as he had been, miserable and barely capable of daily function, but now…. "You seriously had no intention of ever coming to New York with me."

"Don't say that," Samuel said, temper flaring. "New York was always your dream, but I still wanted to go, and when you left—"

"You just had a family already set up," Rory said, unable to stop himself, even though it was essentially a fight they'd had a million times before. "Why would you go with me when you had your parents here, a girl you liked, and a kid on the way?"

"That's not what I was going to say!" Samuel grabbed Rory's upper arm, yanking him forward, and in turn Rory shoved away from him, folding his arms across his chest in defense. "I'm sorry," Samuel said, but the damage was done and Rory turned on his heel, darting inside before Samuel could say anything else.

"WAY TO go, dumbass," Samuel mumbled to himself, digging through his pockets for another cigarette. He smoked the entire thing before heading back inside, finding Juliet pointedly avoiding looking at him as she portioned out cinnamon rolls. "Spit it out," he said, running his fingers back through his hair, still agitated whenever he thought about the look on Rory's face. "Was he crying?"

"No, but he looked like he wanted to, and he gave me a super dirty look," Juliet said, pushing the heel of her palm down on the dough and looking at Samuel. He hated that he only saw pity there. "You need to tell him the truth, Sam."

"He won't listen to me even if I do tell him the truth," Samuel said. "He's upset right now. Is it too much that I expected him to want to see me since he's back in town? He just told me that he had no intention of coming to visit me. If I hadn't bought the lodge, I wouldn't have seen him." He pressed his hands to his face, trying to calm himself down. "Does he really hate me that fucking much?"

"I think it's the opposite," Juliet said. "Are you not scared of being reminded of how much you loved him?"

"No, because I don't need to be reminded," Samuel said quietly. "I never let myself forget about it."

"You should tell him," Juliet said, shaking her head as she sliced off more dough and tossed it into a bowl to rise. "It's not like Rory finding out will do anything other than give him some closure."

"I don't want him to have closure," Samuel said, low and flat. "Having closure means he'll move on, and I don't want that. I know it's selfish, but I always thought he'd come back here and it would just be like nothing had ever happened, that he wouldn't just show up out of the blue with a whole fiancé, acting like it was my fault that he left me behind."

"Well, on his end, that's exactly what happened," Juliet said. "He left nineteen years ago and comes back here to find that you've got an eighteen-year-old son. And you're still wearing that wedding ring. Did you tell Rory about Jamie?"

Samuel looked down at his hand, the gold band on his ring finger, and frowned. "I wear this so I don't have to deal with random guests hitting on me all the time," he said, sighing. "And… I don't know. I feel like the misunderstanding is already too far gone. And Jasper already knew about me and Rory, I guess. He found a picture—"

"Ew," Juliet said, putting her hands up, and Samuel gave her a dirty look. "What?"

"It wasn't anything gross, just one of our last kisses. That's why I kept it. It was a good reminder that things can go from perfect to horrible in less than a day. Guess I don't really need a reminder now, though. He can't stand looking at me. I'm not worried about Jasper. He'll accept me no matter what. But Rory…."

"He deserves to know the truth, Sam," Juliet said. "You've had nineteen years to go looking for him and never did. You can't be upset that he got a fiancé in the meantime."

"Ugh, why are you so reasonable?" Sam asked, groaning. "Why didn't I just hire a bunch of yes-men instead of people with their own opinions?"

"Wait until Clark gets here. He never says no to you," Juliet said.

"Where is he, anyway? It's almost time to get dinner prep underway."

"He had to drop the twins off with my mom, and the weather is kind of shitty," Juliet said, frowning. "We might have to spend the night here, if that's okay with you? I'm not sure we'll be able to get back down to town."

"No, there's no way my two favorite employees can spend the night," Samuel said, sarcasm dripping from his tone. "Just check with Jas and see what rooms are free. It's not like we're particularly busy right now." He glanced toward the door to the kitchen and sighed softly. "I'll talk to Rory when I see him next, but you know what he's like. You saw him in high school."

"Mm, yep, I remember how he'd just become a robot the second he was pissed at you," Juliet said thoughtfully. "I never figured out how you dealt with it."

"Weed," Samuel said, and Juliet laughed. "What? It's true. I don't know if that'll work this time, though."

"Probably not. I think you can figure out another tactic, though, if you really put your mind to it. Now, if you're done with all this misery, can you help me with the cinnamon rolls?"

Chapter Five

THE STORM got worse, and Jasper got more and more bored. At least when Rory had come to the front desk he'd been able to have some company. Instead, all he had now was his sketchbook and the brief appearance of other workers, none of whom wanted to talk to him all that much because they actually had work to do. Even Clark, usually easy to distract, was on a mission when he came in, giving Jasper only the briefest of greetings before making a beeline for the kitchen.

Hours ticked by, and Jasper was almost finished with the book he was reading when the door of the lodge opened and the Caldwells entered, or at least three people who looked reasonably like they could be the Caldwells. The father, tall and elegant; the mother, beautiful and cold; and the son.... Jasper couldn't help but stare, his hazel eyes following the boy. He was Jasper's age, maybe a little bit older, with jet-black hair and porcelain skin, wearing a coat that had clearly been tailored for him and had to be more expensive than Jasper's entire wardrobe combined. He was beautiful, genuinely startlingly beautiful, and Jasper immediately felt horribly ugly and unprepared.

"Good evening," Jasper said, before immediately thinking he sounded like Dracula and turning pink. "Welcome to Evergreen Lodge. My name is Jasper. Can I get your names for check-in?"

"Connor Caldwell," the father said, taking his wallet out of his pocket and giving Jasper a thin-lipped smile. "This is my wife, Cassie, and my son, Louis. I believe we have reservations until the New Year."

Jasper took the man's ID, pulled the reservation up in the system and confirmed the details. "You're in our family suite," he said. "Dinner is served from six to eight each night, with the menu posted every morning. Breakfast is from six to ten, and lunch is from noon to two. Room service is available, and our chef is always happy to make any meals that you might like. We offer shuttle service to town on request as well." He had the entire screed memorized, ensuring the details were correct in the system before handing the ID back to Connor. "How many keys would you like? Three?"

"Three should do fine," Connor said, putting his wallet back in his pocket. "You're the son of the owner, right?"

"Oh," Jasper said, looking startled. "Um, yes. How did you know that?"

"I've met your father in the past," Connor said. "You look just like him. Is he here now?"

"Uh, I think he's helping our chef prepare dinner," Jasper said. "Do you want me to let him know to reach out to you when he's done?" He wasn't sure why, but he was unsettled by the man's question. His dad wasn't exactly a famous hotelier, just a guy who'd bought his local lodge.

"That would be perfect," Connor said, taking the keys from him. "What room are we in?"

"The room number is 306," Jasper said. "The elevators are right over there past the Christmas tree." He paused, remembering what he'd forgotten to mention. "Oh, of course! On Saturday, we have a tree-decorating event. We'll be holding holiday events in the run-up to the big day. It's sort of our town's thing."

"Oh, we've heard," Cassie said, speaking up for the first time. Jasper was surprised to find that her English was heavily accented, most likely French. "It's quite charming. Thanks for everything, sweetheart. Come along, boys."

Jasper blinked, watching them go, only to be caught off guard by Louis looking back over his shoulder and meeting his gaze. His eyes were dark, intense, and a chill went through Jasper that he didn't think had anything to do with the snow outside. It was made worse when Louis smiled at him, Jasper clutching the edge of the counter and wondering just what the hell the Caldwells were doing here. It wasn't as though they had the fanciest lodge in the state, certainly not fancy enough for people who had just flown in from Paris and dressed like *that*.

And Louis… fuck. Jasper avoided crushes like the plague, mostly because he had seen what Rory had left behind and didn't want to do the same. A crush on a random guest was not good. He'd have to tamp that down no matter what. He pretended he was doing something on the computer so Louis would stop looking at him, and when he looked back over, the elevator doors were opening and the Caldwells were going in, the blond who'd arrived with Rory on his way out.

Jasper stared at the man for a few long seconds before turning back to his computer, hoping against hope that—Martel? Mario? Something like that—just needed something from his car and wasn't coming over to bother him. His hopes were dashed when the man appeared in front of him, looking at Jasper closely. Jasper pretended to type something on the computer before looking up, schooling his expression into one of total innocence. "Can I help you, sir?"

"I'm thirty-two, don't call me sir."

"My apologies, you look much older," Jasper said, continuing with the cherub act he used whenever there were rude guests. It usually meant they felt too bad to yell at him and instead meant they yelled at his father, which suited him fine. "Did you need something? We have room service."

The vaguest hint of discomfort passed over the man's handsome face, and he sighed, glancing past Jasper to the kitchen doors before turning his attention back the front desk. Jasper was busy pulling up Rory's room to see if the guy's name was in the notes when the man spoke, something monotone in his voice. "I've been told that I need to apologize to you," he said, the words like pulling teeth. "So… here's my apology."

Jasper waited, but the guy said nothing else, gave no further indication that he was going to say anything else, and Jasper blinked. "What? Dude, that wasn't an apology! Saying you need to apologize, and then not saying anything else isn't an apology."

"I don't want to apologize to you, though." Malcolm—his name thankfully on the account—was looking at him with that same haughty look as earlier, and Jasper wondered which one of them was the teenager and which was the adult. "Rory said I had to, but I don't understand why."

"Did you not clarify with Rory?" Jasper asked, frowning. He wondered if this was indirectly his father's doing. When Rory had returned from their conversation earlier, he had looked the picture of misery.

Malcolm rolled his eyes, clearly irritated. "I'm assuming he thought I was rude earlier when I said you were slow."

"I was trying to see if I could switch your room so you guys could share a bed," Jasper said, and he was pleased to see that Malcolm seemed surprised by that admission. "So I think you're correct."

"Then I apologize for saying you were slow. I was in a bad mood from driving all day, and I was wrong to take it out on you."

"So you do know how to apologize! That's good."

"Don't push your luck," Malcolm said, although Jasper thought there was the barest hint of amusement to his voice now. "What do you know about your dad and Rory?"

"What? Don't ask me that, ask Rory," Jasper said. "I'm not your friend."

"Obviously I'm not friends with a child working at a hotel," Malcolm said, his haughtiness returning, and Jasper rolled his eyes.

"I'm eighteen, weirdo."

"Oh, my apologies. Then I'm just not your friend."

"Then ask your fiancé about my dad," Jasper shot back. "Didn't you ask him about his past when you got engaged?"

"It didn't come up," Malcolm said flatly. He scanned the lobby, sparsely inhabited at this time of day, and Jasper got the distinct impression he was trying to avoid going back to his room. Maybe they'd gotten in a fight over his dad. Jasper kind of hoped that was the case; it was kind of romantic to think about. "Who's that?"

"Who?" Jasper asked, leaning over the desk and following Malcolm's gaze to Ty, who was standing with the lens of his camera pressed against one of the huge windows that overlooked the town down below. "The guy with the camera?"

"Yes."

"I can't give you the personal information for another guest," Jasper said, oozing with fake politeness. "But you're free to go ask yourself."

"You're kind of useless, huh?"

"Maybe you're just asking weird stuff."

Malcolm rapped his knuckles against the front desk, looking Jasper dead in the face, and Jasper was struck both by how handsome he was and how snake-like his eyes were. "I'll give you twenty dollars."

"No! Go talk to him or I'll tell Rory you're trying to hit on another guy in front of me."

Malcolm frowned, seeming to weigh the pros and cons before deciding it wasn't worth it. "Fine," he said, turning on his heel and walking over to Ty.

TRUTHFULLY, MALCOLM recognized him. Or at least he was pretty sure he recognized him. If he wasn't mistaken, the man currently taking pictures out the lodge window was the same man who had done the photography for one of their new skyscrapers the year before in Manhattan. It was strange to see him here, wearing a college sweater and a pair of paint-stained jeans instead of a suit, but Malcolm had felt a strange little thrill when he'd seen him, not that he would ever admit it out loud.

He knew what sort of man he was. Attraction was something he kept under wraps, a fatal weakness that he could not afford thanks to his ambition, but Ty—if it was truly Ty—had caught his eye the year before and caught his eye again now. Malcolm walked up alongside him, looking outside with his hands in the pockets of his trousers. It really was beautiful here. He had left Rory alone to begin working on plans, although he had also gotten the distinct impression that something had happened while he'd been asleep and Rory didn't want him in the room if it was at all possible.

Malcolm took in the view for a few more moments before looking over at Ty, who was still taking pictures and seemed to either not know he was there or didn't care. "Excuse me," Malcolm said, resting his shoulder against the glass as he turned to face Ty head-on. "Are you Ty Choi, by chance?"

Ty, whose face had almost immediately turned sour as he was distracted from his camera, softened a bit as he heard his name. The last of the irritation fell away as he saw Malcolm, recognition clear in his dark eyes. "I know you," he said, letting his camera hang from the strap around his neck and digging through his pockets before removing a comically overstuffed wallet. He thumbed through it quickly and removed a familiar business card, although it was decidedly more creased than it had been when Malcolm had given it to him. "Malcolm DuPont, Architect."

"What? How did you remember that was my card? Your wallet is full."

"I only keep the business cards of the cute ones," Ty said, catching Malcolm entirely off guard. "You're very unique, which helps. I remember your blond eyelashes."

Malcolm's heart gave that traitorous little lurch again. He knew he was handsome. It was something he had never questioned, but for someone to compliment something so specific, something as insignificant as his eyelashes… it surprised him. "What are you doing here?"

"My brother-in-law works for a production company, and they're looking to shoot a Christmas movie next summer, but I wanted to see if I can find a small town to film in that looks cute enough. I'm scouting locations, but I was supposed to be staying in town. That boy at the front desk saved my hide."

Malcolm glanced at Jasper, who was watching them like a hawk, and wondered what the teenager would report to Rory. It wasn't as though they were actually engaged, but if he wanted Rory to withdraw from the partnership competition, he needed to keep up his end of the bargain. "He doesn't like me very much."

"Hm, I can see how you could rub some people the wrong way," Ty said. "Luckily for you, I'm immune to brusque men. So what are you doing here? I doubt you're scouting a Christmas movie."

"I'm here to evaluate if this lodge is a business my firm wants to acquire," Malcolm said. "Since they have a reputation for their Christmas events, I'm here for Christmas." He looked out the window again, at the snow falling in large flakes over the trees and road that wound down the mountain. "Maybe that's why the kid doesn't like me."

"No, I think it's probably your tone," Ty said, grinning at him, and Malcolm was almost tempted to smile back. "I really was struck by your looks when we first met. This might seem forward, but if you get bored with architecture during your stay, I'd like to photograph you." He lifted his camera again, peering at Malcolm through the viewfinder. "Mm, in a black turtleneck, honestly. Do you have glasses?"

"You want me to be your Barbie?"

"Sweet man, you don't want to open that door to me," Ty said, dropping his camera again. "I would love to dress you up, but right now I have to go get dressed for dinner. Apparently it's a very big affair when there are so few guests."

Like that, he was gone, Malcolm watching him disappear up the stairs and feeling… very strange, to be honest. He had found Ty attractive from a distance at the event last year, but now, up close, he found him ridiculously charismatic. It was rare to find someone who ignored his attitude and saw through to the underneath, but Ty had cut through it with ease. Even Rory, who he'd worked with for years, still found him irritating on the daily.

He was contemplating what to do when he realized someone was hissing at him. Malcolm looked over to find Jasper gesturing at him animatedly, and as soon as he walked back over to the desk the teenager smacked him hard on the arm. "Hey, whoa, you can't just hit an adult like that."

"Why are you flirting with another man?" Jasper hissed. "Are you seriously that shameless?"

Malcolm looked at him, Jasper's face flushed pink like he'd just seen something he shouldn't have, and considered it for a moment. "Tell Rory if you want," he said finally. "That man did photography for us in the city, so I was just catching up. Rory knows him as well. You really shouldn't be getting this upset on behalf of someone you don't know, by the way."

"But I do know Rory," Jasper said, frowning. "Or at least my dad does."

"Does he? He didn't know what firm he was at, or who he's marrying, or that he was coming here. That doesn't sound like two people who know each other anymore." He tilted his head to one side, looking at Jasper with some curiosity. "Based on your age, I'd say that you're probably the reason they don't know each other. I'm sure the thought has crossed your mind before. See you at dinner."

He left before Jasper could say anything in return, the teenager clearly offput by what Malcolm had said, but Malcolm didn't think his observation was news to the kid. He had to realize that his age matched up pretty well with Rory's exodus from Evergreen Hill, whether he was the cause or merely an effect. He let himself into the room to find Rory still at the desk, a novel's worth of paperwork scattered around him as he made notes on each page. "Dinner will be soon," he said, glancing at Rory when he didn't immediately respond. "Do you have your headphones in?"

"I'm going to skip dinner," Rory said, rubbing his forehead and looking over at Malcolm, who looked back at him unflinchingly. "What?"

"Why did you come here if you were just going to mope up in your room the entire time? I don't want to be the one who has to talk to everyone. I'm not good at it. You can't avoid that guy forever."

"I'm not avoiding him. I just… I just don't want to see him tonight."

"Listen to me," Malcolm said, sitting down on the edge of his bed and watching Rory, who looked at him more out of surprise at his tone than anything else. "Pretending to be your fiancé is extremely inconvenient, and I don't think that you're acting rationally. Why don't you just talk to him?"

"Because I don't want to come into his life and ruin it again," Rory said. "He's got a son and a wife. He clearly moved on from me. It's not fair for me to expect him to give that stuff up for me."

"Are you sure he has a wife? I mean, he's wearing a wedding ring, but I haven't seen her, and that kid on the front desk hasn't mentioned her."

"I'm positive," Rory said. "Her name is Juliet. We went to high school together." He felt sick just saying it out loud and turned back to his blueprints. "I'm sorry. I'll think of something to do, just... I don't think I can do it right away."

"Fine," Malcolm said, frowning. "But I think you're only going to feel worse in the long run."

Chapter Six

"DAD, YOU have to go up there and talk to him."

Samuel sighed, rubbing at his forehead as a steady headache pulsed just behind his eyes. It had been three days since Rory had abruptly reappeared in his life and three days of feeling like someone had put his chest in a vise, made a hundred times worse by the fact that Rory had been steadfastly avoiding him since that first day. His fiancé was taking full advantage of the meals at the lodge, but Rory himself was just ordering room service, seemingly avoiding any parts of the hotel where Samuel might be. The worst part was that it hurt. It actually fucking hurt, thinking that Rory would rather seal himself up in a hotel room than come talk to him, and Samuel had spent several sleepless nights trying to figure out exactly what he was supposed to do. "I can't," he finally said, his voice barely audible.

"You have to," Jasper said, drizzling icing on a scone and looking at his dad, concern written all over his face. One of the other seasonal workers was at the front desk, and Jasper had agreed to help Juliet with the baking, although he wasn't exactly the best sous chef, considering the amount of flour currently dusted all over his hands and jeans. "I'm not spending Christmas with you miserable like this, okay? It's awful."

"I'm not miserable."

"Whatever! You're not happy, I can see that much. Now's your opportunity to go and talk to him without that Scottish guy there bothering him." He shoved the plate of scones at his dad, raising his eyebrows. "Go upstairs."

"Where's Malcolm?"

"He's been flirting with Ty since he spotted him," Jasper said. "I don't know what his endgame is, but Ty's falling for it. I don't understand why everyone in this hotel is acting like they don't know how to communicate."

"Oh, so you finally managed to talk to Louis Caldwell?" Samuel asked, and Jasper turned pink before shaking his head in embarrassment. "I'll go, but you need to try and talk to that kid."

"Okay, okay," Jasper said. "Get going before you lose your window of opportunity. I'll text you if that guy stops trying to cheat on his fiancé and heads upstairs."

"I guess when you have a kid you get a built-in wingman," Samuel said, looking down at the scones and trying to get the nerve up before leaving the kitchen and heading for the stairs. He spotted Malcolm and Ty, the pair of them hunched over one of the tables in the sitting area with a group of photos laid out before them, and decided to give the guy the benefit of the doubt. Ty was from New York, Malcolm was from New York, and so far they'd really just been looking at pictures together. It seemed more likely that Malcolm was getting Ty's opinion on some construction project, mostly because the idea of anyone willfully cheating on a man like Rory was totally foreign to Samuel.

He wondered if this was how it felt to be on death row, walking down that long hall to the electrocution chair at the end, but that wasn't fair to Rory. God, he missed the days where he could trust Rory with anything, could love him wholeheartedly, but those teenagers were so far removed from the men they were now that it seemed a total impossibility to return to that sort of relationship.

The room they'd given the pair was at the end of the second-floor hallway overlooking the town, a suite usually given to people who were staying for an extended period of time because it had a separate sitting area. Sickness washed over Samuel as he approached the door, his grip on the plate of scones tightening to the point where he thought he might shatter the ceramic, and he had to remind himself to settle down. He didn't want to see Rory and Malcolm's little all-inclusive love nest.

He stood in front of the door for a few long moments, trying to ignore the dozen or so miserable thoughts racing through his mind. He could just go back downstairs. Toss the scones at Malcolm and Ty, get on his ATV, head down the mountain to his parents' house and cry in his childhood bed the way he had when Rory had first left. But that would set a terrible example for Jasper, and he wasn't going to let that happen.

Finally, he mustered up the courage to knock.

"Jesus Christ," he heard Rory swear on the other side of the door. "How many times are you going to forget your fucking key? Why did we have them give us two if—"

The door swung open, Rory standing on the other side in just a pair of sweatpants. Like a gay—gayer?—Sherlock Holmes, Samuel quickly scanned Rory's appearance, his heart stuttering in his chest. Sweatpants that didn't look like they fit him properly, sitting just a little too low on his hips so the bones were visible. Chintzy black glasses that were way too dorky but looked cute on Rory, although Samuel knew he shouldn't be having that thought. Rory had stayed slim as an adult, his body once a map that Samuel had memorized, and there were still familiar landmarks, like the two-shades-lighter scar that cut across the right side of his torso where Rory had fallen off his bike as a kid.

He had changed but he hadn't, the sheer fucking beauty of him hitting Samuel so hard in the stomach he thought he might pass out. Samuel just barely opened his mouth to speak when he realized Rory was staring at him like he'd been punched too, and before Samuel could say anything, Rory was slamming the door closed. "Hey," Samuel said, the word barely a croak. "Hey!"

An endless silence, and then Rory opened the door again, this time just the barest crack. He was looking at Samuel, dark eyes reflecting Samuel's own nerves right back at him. "What do you want?" he asked, and Samuel noticed he was gripping the edge of the door tightly.

"I brought you some scones," Samuel said, holding up the plate. "Can I come in?"

"Uh, no," Rory said, and Samuel raised a hand to push against the door lightly. "Don't do that."

"I'm coming in," Samuel said and pushed the door open, Rory backing up and glaring at him. Samuel glanced around the room, taking in the fact that one bed was disheveled and one was perfectly made— they were sleeping together, obviously—and that the floor was covered in blueprints. "You're actually working up here?"

"Of course I am," Rory said, frowning intently and making his way through the labyrinth of bare floor to grab a sweater off the disheveled bed. He tugged it on and turned back to Samuel, arms crossed over his chest. "What did you think I was doing up here?"

"Avoiding me," Samuel said, setting the scones down on top of the dresser. "Because you're scared of me, or…. Or worse, because you genuinely don't want to see me." Rory ducked his head, steadfastly staring at the ground, and Samuel continued. "I don't know why you're acting like this, but I don't want you to spend the next week just hiding up in your room. We need to clear the air."

"You shouldn't be in here," Rory said, keeping his distance, although Samuel could see that he was constantly looking at the plate of scones. They were cranberry lemon, and Samuel *knew* that Rory liked the combination, had specifically requested them to try and tempt Rory into talking to him, but if he had been betting on Rory's stubbornness abating at all in the intervening years, it was abundantly clear that it had not. "Malcolm might misunderstand."

"I left the door open," Samuel said. He wasn't going to take any of Rory's excuses, would continue to batter at his defenses until he had to lower his walls. "And he's downstairs with Ty right now. They looked busy."

"The photographer," Rory said, lifting a hand to his lips to chew at his thumbnail. A flash of jealousy went through Samuel, and he forced himself to let it go, reminding himself that he was just here to make amends so they could both get through Christmas without incident. It was none of his business whether Malcolm was cheating on Rory or not. He would never do it, but Rory had made his choice, and if he wanted to be engaged to a guy who so clearly had feelings for someone else, that was his business. "Fine. Say what you want to say and then leave. I'm obviously busy."

Samuel hadn't really expected to get this far. He had nineteen years of stuff to say, and none of it seemed to want to come out, all of it sticking in his throat like dry toast, which wasn't the most romantic metaphor but had to do. Rory stared at him expectantly, and Samuel couldn't figure out if it was irritation in his dark eyes or frustration that neither of them seemed capable of saying anything. "I missed you," Samuel finally said, and Rory recoiled. "Don't act like that."

"Like what?" Rory bit out. So it was irritation after all. "Like you have no right to have missed me when you're the one who separated us?"

"Is that the way you see it?" Samuel asked, trying to keep the bitterness out of his own voice, trying to stay calm and objective despite how Rory's words had hit him directly in the heart. "That it was my fault we've been apart for this long? Jesus, Rory, do you not remember that time at all? You're the one who decided he had to up and leave all of a sudden. You're the one who wanted to go to New York and become an architect, and I would have supported you in all that, but—"

"But what?"

"But you never asked me! You never fucking asked if I wanted to go with you! You just assumed that I would pick up and leave with you without taking me into consideration at all!" Samuel realized he was yelling and stopped himself, dragging a hand over his face, flushed red from anger. "I wasn't ready to leave, but I didn't want to hold you back. I thought… I thought maybe we could do a year apart, but… but things obviously changed. And I never told you that I was scared of leaving and that I wanted to stay with my parents for a while longer. I never wanted to go to the city."

Rory was looking at him now, his brow furrowed intently as he listened, but Samuel could tell just from the way he was holding himself that he was caught up in his own thoughts. A sudden, unfriendly feeling that Rory had never truly listened to him overcame him, and Samuel briefly considered fleeing the room, giving up on this, but the way his heart hurt when he looked at Rory told him it wasn't the right thing to do. "I bought you a bus ticket."

"I know."

"I didn't stay in the dorms that first year because I had rented an apartment for us with my scholarship money and what I'd saved from the tree farm," Rory continued, his voice flat, robotic, like these were facts he had been holding on to for years and had just begun to put together properly. "Your parents kept sending me money for food."

"I know," Samuel repeated. "I told them to. You only ever ate enough for you to survive, and I didn't want to think about you in the city starving to death."

"Fuck you," Rory snapped, Samuel realizing too late he'd misjudged that look in his eyes. It wasn't just irritation, it was anger, the sort of anger Rory had rarely ever turned on him, which was why Samuel hadn't been able to see it before. "You should have been there instead of hiding behind money. You should have been with me! I left Evergreen because I didn't have any family here, and—"

"What are you even saying?" Samuel said, temper flaring again. "No family? I was your family. My parents loved you like their own kid, and I… fuck, Rory, you have no clue how much I loved you or you never would have left me, not ever. You knew I wasn't ready, but you left anyway. You knew me better than anyone. You must have known I wasn't ready to go."

Rory mumbled something, and Samuel stepped closer to him, splaying his arms to either side. "What?"

"You weren't my family," Rory said, a little louder, and then he was stepping back over the blueprints and shoving Samuel toward the door of the room. "You weren't my family when you were getting Juliet pregnant and leaving me alone in that fucking city."

"What? Juliet—"

"Just shut up!" Rory snapped, shoving him harder, and Samuel stumbled, careening into the hallway. "Don't come up here again, Samuel. I don't have anything left to say to you."

He slammed the door behind Samuel, who was left reeling. "Juliet?" he whispered, rubbing at his jaw. "What the fuck is he talking about?"

Chapter Seven

RORY HAD always liked the hour just before dawn.

It was quiet, few people out and about in Evergreen, and normally Rory would be catching a ride in Samuel's truck, heading for a shift at Craig's tree farm, the tree farm where he'd spent the last three summers earning enough money to make today possible. Because today was *not* normal; it was the start of something new and exciting, and just thinking about it was making his heart race.

He was the only one at the bus station, settled on a bench just outside to greet the dawn despite how humid it was already. His duffel bag, beaten from years of use, was sitting alongside him, stuffed to the brim with the most important pieces of his life, everything else left behind in his bedroom at his grandparents' house. He wouldn't need it again, New York City promising a new life with new things, and what he'd brought was just enough to keep him going for another week or two: toothbrush, underwear, a few of Samuel's sweaters....

Rory grinned, his face warm with more than just the creeping summer heat, and checked the pair of bus tickets held in his hand, slightly crumpled from how tightly he'd been gripping them. Seats H1 and H2, side by side so they could hold hands if they wanted to, Samuel by the window because he liked to watch the world go by when he wasn't driving. They'd been expensive, but that was okay, a down payment on a future together that Rory had spent his teenage years hurtling toward, every bit of hard work paying off.

He'd gotten into NYU, found a tiny studio apartment that was affordable with his limited budget and the cafe job he'd already secured, thanks to a friend of Samuel's parents, and he was leaving Evergreen behind with Samuel well in hand. He had never been more sure about the trajectory of his life.

But the bus left at five thirty, and it was five twenty-five now.

Samuel was the sort of guy to show up early everywhere he went, chronically punctual. They'd gone on bus trips before, and he'd never arrived later than fifteen minutes prior to the bus leaving, and even that arrival had been too late for his comfort. Leaving it to five minutes was insanity, honestly, totally out of character. Maybe there was something wrong with his truck? The thing was old, and even with all his mechanical know-how, Samuel could sometimes be stumped. His parents must be dropping him off, maybe his sister. He'd be here.

The bus pulled up, and Rory watched the passengers file off, the bus sparsely populated for this trip. Evergreen was the last stop on the New York City circuit before it turned around, and at this time of year it wasn't the popular tourist destination it became as winter began to descend. Rory didn't stir, though, scanning the parking lot for a sign of Samuel, his heart clutched in a vise.

Headlights came down the road that connected the station to town, and relief washed over Rory. He grabbed the strap of his bag and got to his feet, hoisting the duffel over his shoulder so he could put it in the storage compartment. The vehicle in the parking lot found a spot—weird, but maybe Samuel's parents wanted to say goodbye to him too—and then the headlights went dead.

The only person who emerged was an older man Rory had never seen before, the guy clambering aboard the bus with a backpack and nothing else. "Hey, kid," the bus driver said, standing near a column smoking. "If you're not on the bus before I'm done with this cigarette, I leave without you."

"I'm just waiting for a friend," Rory said, showing the man both bus tickets. "He should be here any moment."

"I'm on a strict schedule," the driver said, waving his hand. "When you bought the tickets, it was made clear that we wouldn't detour from the schedule even in the case of late arrivals."

This time it was sickness that washed over Rory, an awful sour taste in his mouth as he approached the bus and stuck his duffel in the open storage compartment. He looked at the parking lot again, but nothing had changed, no headlights coming down the drive. The bus driver coughed behind him, and Rory realized he was out of time, that five thirty had come and Samuel had not.

He got on the bus, keeping a tight grip on both tickets as he headed for his seat. By the time he reached it he was crying, settling into the window seat and pressing the heels of his palms to his face, the perforated end of the ticket rough against his skin as he refused to let it go. There was still a chance, still the possibility that Samuel would show up last minute, burst onto the bus with that goofy lopsided smile of his, tell him he was sorry.

The bus began to move.

Chapter Eight

RORY GROANED, dragging his hand over his face and staring up at the ceiling of the hotel room. It had been so long since he'd had that dream that he thought maybe he'd forgotten how it felt to be on that bus, to realize Samuel wasn't coming, but it seemed like being back in Evergreen was dredging up every last emotion he'd wanted so badly to bury.

He rolled onto his side, looking out the window at the clear blue sky, the snow no longer falling. Yesterday morning he'd been working on blueprints when Samuel had appeared, and…. God, he'd been such an asshole. He wasn't even really sure what had happened after that. He'd spent the rest of the day angrily working, but at some point he must have fallen asleep.

"Are you up?"

Rory rolled over the other way, finding Malcolm standing between the two beds and looking down at him, impeccably dressed as always… although for some reason he was currently wearing a genuine Christmas sweater. Tasteful, of course, but still a Christmas sweater, with a little snowman and everything. Rory sat up straight, looking at him with sheer confusion. "What are you wearing?"

"Is that the thanks I get for putting you in the bed instead of letting you sleep on top of your blueprints?" Malcolm asked, rolling up his sleeves just enough to show off his forearms. He looked at Rory, something unfamiliar in his usually icy gaze—pity? Jesus, that was the worst. "I'm worried about you."

"I'm fine," Rory said, sighing softly. "Thanks for not leaving me on the floor."

"I'm so magnanimous," Malcolm said, frowning down at him. "Samuel came up here yesterday and came down about ten minutes later crying, and then I found you passed out on the floor with an untouched plate of scones on the dresser. I don't know what happened to you and him, Rory, not really, but it's becoming increasingly difficult to explain why my fiancé has locked himself in our room and refuses to eat meals with everyone else."

"I'm so stupid," Rory said. "I told him we weren't family, that I just expected him to come with me, and he would have done it too. And you should have seen his face when I accused him of getting Juliet pregnant. Why do I feel bad about the truth?"

"Juliet…," Malcolm said, his forehead crinkling briefly before he shook his head. "Listen. Whoever the Samuel downstairs is, he's not the Samuel that you left behind twenty years ago, just like you're not the same Rory. I'm not saying you should just throw yourself at him, but… try to work things out. Anyway, I just wanted to make sure you were breathing and change my sweater. I have a date."

"A date?" Rory asked. "But you're my fiancé."

"And your fiancé is extremely interested in spending time with Ty Choi," Malcolm said, looking almost dreamy as he said it. "He has to photograph the town for work today, so I said I would go with him to do research on local businesses. And if I end up buying him a gingerbread latte, well… that's okay too." His gaze hardened again, and he looked at Rory. "This engagement needs to be called off by Christmas Eve, because I have never met someone more willing to put up with me."

"Maybe you shouldn't be expecting people to just put up with you," Rory said, but he waved his hand when Malcolm opened his mouth again. "I'm joking. Go on your date. I'll… I'll go talk to Samuel."

"Good. And watch out for his kid, because I think public opinion might be against you since you made Samuel cry." With that Malcolm grabbed his cross-body bag and headed for the door, then closed it behind him. It took Rory forever to get out of bed, both because of how warm it was and how little he wanted to go downstairs and apologize to both Samuel and Jasper for how he'd been acting, but he finally managed to drag himself out of bed and to the shower.

The hot water did wonders for him, tidying up his blueprints and pulling on a clean set of clothes even more, and he was soon feeling more human than he had all week. Facing Samuel seemed doable now, although not pleasant, and Rory wondered if he could overcome his pride and admit that he had missed him, even if things would never go back to the way they had once been. Truthfully, seeing Samuel that first day had filled him with hope, a hunger like he hadn't felt in decades, and if he hadn't seen the wedding ring, he didn't think things would be as suffocating as they were now.

But he couldn't expect someone to hang around for him for twenty years.

He sighed and left the room, taking the stairs down to the entrance hall. Jasper was standing halfway up a huge ladder, holding lights in his arms and looking down at a kid Rory hadn't seen before. The pair of them were joking and laughing together until Jasper saw Rory, at which point he stopped and looked at him. Rory was expecting a barrage of insults or just a flat-out refusal to speak to him, but instead Jasper grinned at the dark-haired boy holding the other end of the string of lights. "You owe me twenty bucks, Louis."

"Why?" Louis asked, looking back at Rory and groaning. "Oh, shit."

"What kind of reaction is that?" Rory asked, walking over to them and looking up at the tree. "I thought you were decorating this tomorrow?"

"We are, but we have to string the lights first," Jasper said, getting back to the arduous task. "And Louis and I had a bet. He thought my dad killed you and that's why he was crying yesterday. But I figured you guys just had a stupid fight."

"It was just a stupid fight," Rory agreed. "He was actually crying? I thought Malcolm was just saying that to make me feel bad."

"He cries when he gets frustrated," Jasper said, and Rory smiled— so he hadn't outgrown that. "He's in the kitchen if you want to go talk to him."

"He spends a lot of time in there, huh?"

"He's technically the pastry chef," Jasper said. "But that's just because he enjoys it. If you hurry you should be able to catch him."

"Catch him?" Rory echoed, but he didn't stay any longer, heading toward the kitchen despite his trepidation. He didn't catch the look Louis and Jasper gave one another behind his back, or the grin that split across Jasper's face as he went back to stringing lights.

Samuel was standing near the oven, deep in conversation with Juliet, and Rory regretted coming in for a brief moment before Juliet tapped Samuel on the arm and pointed in his direction. Any chance of running back out was lost, but instead of Samuel looking at him with anger or sorrow, Rory found that he was grinning. "Hey!" Samuel called, coming around the counter. "You got here in the nick of time."

"What's going on?" Rory asked, looking mildly surprised. "Jasper said something about catching you too."

"I'm heading to town to get some stuff for tomorrow's Christmas tree decorating," Samuel said, grabbed a notepad off the counter and stuffed it in his pocket. "Malcolm said he'd wake you up so you could come with me."

"Oh, he said that, did he?" Rory asked, amused despite himself. So Malcolm was appointing himself wingman after all. It wasn't surprising after what he'd said this morning—Rory remembered Ty from the event the year before and had to admit that the guy was handsome. It was fair to assume that the sooner he and Samuel sorted stuff out, the sooner Malcolm would be able to properly woo Ty. "It would be nice to go and see some of the old spots," he admitted. "Have things changed a lot?"

"A fair bit, yeah," Samuel said, and he was acting like their fight hadn't happened, like Rory hadn't said those terrible things. God, Samuel had always been like that. Even when they'd fight in high school, Samuel was always the one who would come and apologize first. Rory had never met someone less able to hold grudges, if he was being honest. "Are Jasper and Louis still putting the lights on the tree?"

"Yeah, they apparently had a bet on whether I'd come down or not," Rory said, and Samuel laughed. God, Rory had missed that sound. Samuel was *so* important to him. Maybe it was okay if they were just friends now. Maybe it meant he could keep Samuel in his life despite the implosion of their previous romantic relationship. The fact that his heart hurt every time he caught sight of the wedding ring was irrelevant. "I'm ready to go if you are."

"Sounds good," Samuel said. "Let's go out the back way. I promised Jasper I wouldn't embarrass him."

"Oh, he's on a date with that kid?"

"Not a date, but, uh… I don't know," Samuel said, leading Rory down the hall toward the old servants' quarters and the exit beyond. "Jas feels too responsible, honestly, and he doesn't take the time to really do stuff for himself. I encouraged him to ask Louis to hang out. Even if nothing comes of it, it'll still be good for him to make a friend."

"He sounds a lot like you," Rory said, stepping through the door as Samuel held it open for him. It was cold out, the sky an endless blue, and Rory pulled his coat further around his shoulders, smiling at Samuel. "Too responsible for his age and involved in the family business."

"Yeah, he definitely got a lot of that," Samuel said, unlocking a blue pickup truck with snow chains on the wheels. "It's kind of crazy how much like me he is, all things considered. I'd figured he'd take after his mom more."

"Yeah, you were always more like your mom," Rory said, climbing into the passenger seat. "How are your parents doing, by the way? We drove past the bed and breakfast on the way up."

"They're doing well," Samuel said as he got in the driver's side, smiling at Rory. A distinct feeling of being unworthy of his forgiveness overcame Rory, guilt at what he'd said the day before striking him right in the heart once again. "Dad still owns the farm, but he can't really get out there and work on it as much as he used to. Jasper and I can help in the summer to some extent, but… I'm kind of thinking of buying it and incorporating it into the lodge. Give them their retirement."

"So the lodge is doing well?" Rory asked, mostly because he was unable to say the stuff he actually wanted to say—that he had missed Samuel, that he had lied about Malcolm out of sheer panic, that he would give anything to be just a miniscule part of Samuel's life again. The words all died in his throat, and all he could ask were the meaningless little questions that Samuel had undoubtedly answered a million times before.

"For sure," Samuel said, the truck doing surprisingly well on the roads despite the snow that had entrenched them for the past few days. "We're still not into the busiest time of year, but once January hits, we get slammed. And we do pretty well during the off-season too, because it's not like there's just skiing around here. There's hiking too, swimming, just general summer stuff."

"It does get beautiful in the summer," Rory said, watching the snow-covered landscape pass them by as they headed down the mountain. He'd always liked winter best—curling up in sweaters, drinking hot chocolate, having an excuse to hibernate. He looked back at Samuel, about to say more, but Samuel grinned and shook his head.

"You don't have to pretend around me, Ror. I know you've always been a sucker for winter. Do you remember the year it snowed on Halloween? I was so upset because I had to wear a coat over my *Top Gun* costume, but you were just thrilled as could be and wanted to go sledding instead of getting candy. What kind of lunatic wants to skip trick-or-treating to go play in the snow?"

Rory couldn't help but laugh at the memory, shaking his head. "And your parents took me sledding right after we were done," he said. "Even though it was way past our bedtimes on a school night." He paused, rubbing at his mouth briefly. "I'm sorry for what I said yesterday," he said finally. "I shouldn't have told you that I didn't have family here. Your parents always looked after me. *You* always looked after me. I was just pissed. It's not an excuse, but it's the truth, unfortunately."

"It stung," Samuel said after a moment of thought, drumming his fingers against the steering wheel. "I was pretty upset, I won't lie. I'm sure, uh, Jas told you I was crying. And I was, but it wasn't because of what you said, not really. I just couldn't stop thinking that I hadn't done enough to convince you that we were family when you were still here and that's why you left after all."

"That wasn't why I left," Rory said. "I said it yesterday because I wanted to hurt you, but it was immature and stupid. I really just left because I wanted to become an architect, and I wanted to prove I could make something of myself. I never thought I'd stay away so long." It was the truth, plain and simple. Rory had always figured he'd make his way back after graduation. He just didn't think it would take him nearly twenty years. "I didn't mean to."

"Time has a funny way of creeping up on you," Samuel said as they reached the downtown core and parked on the side of the road in front of the local grocery store. "But you can make it up to me with some physical labor, luckily. I'm easy to please."

"Oh, you're enlisting me for help? I'm a city boy now, Sam. I don't think I'm very good at physical labor."

"Good thing it's just pushing a cart," Samuel said, grinning at him and punching him lightly on the shoulder. They clambered out of the truck and headed into the store, Rory following Samuel closely.

They spent nearly an hour in the store, Samuel carefully picking out ingredients while Rory trailed after him with the cart, observing the other man closely. It seemed like everyone they passed in the aisles knew him, which wasn't exactly a surprise, but Samuel treated them all like they were bosom friends and chatted with each about their family, their plans for Christmas, and more. It was almost painful after a while, seeing how much everyone adored Samuel, how much he'd grown to be an integral part of Evergreen while Rory had been away.

The groceries purchased and the truck loaded up, Samuel grinned at Rory. "Coffee and croissant?"

"Is Pat's still open?"

"Yep! And she gives me a discount because she loves me so much." Samuel paused, rubbing the side of his neck. "Is it more impressive if I don't get a discount? Whatever. Come on, it's on me."

Rory fell into step alongside Samuel as they made their way down the sidewalk toward the cafe, their mere proximity enough to awaken so many old memories. They'd walked this exact path a hundred times before, their hands close enough for their skin to brush. Even now Rory wondered what would happen if he dipped his hand into Samuel's, held it the way he had once loved to do, kissed his knuckles. It was a temptation he couldn't allow himself to give in to.

Chapter Nine

PAT'S, SITUATED on Main Street in an old building that had been an inn before the town had ever been established, looked much the same as Rory remembered it: an old stone building with freshly painted red trim, the front window lovingly hand painted with a dozen or so ornaments and snowmen. "Wow," Rory said, standing on the edge of the sidewalk to take in the sight of the cafe. "It really hasn't changed much at all."

"No," Samuel agreed, looking up at the building as well, in order to appreciate it alongside Rory. "Do you remember when I crashed my bike into the front of the cafe?"

"Yeah, and you cried for, like, fifteen minutes while I tried to get you to eat a croissant?" Rory shot back, pushing open the front door of the cafe and holding it for Samuel. "I was so embarrassed for you."

"Seriously? That's so mean," Samuel said, laughing as he followed Rory inside. "I had a skinned knee!"

"You absolutely did not," Rory said. "You weren't bleeding at all, man." The cafe was busy but not crowded, bustling with tourists and locals alike, and both the sight and smell of it was comforting to Rory. Freshly baked pastries mingled with the scent of coffee and hot chocolate, the sweetness of the air familiar even after decades away. The girl behind the counter immediately recognized Samuel, and after ordering two croissants and two drinks—an americano for Rory and a candy cane mocha for Samuel—they found a booth by the front window.

Rory settled into the seat, looking out to the street at the bustle of everyday Evergreen Hill life. Despite the surface-level changes, the growth of some big-name corporations in the town, the individuality of the place was still apparent. Rory was used to his haunts in New York, but he was surprised to find that he was still accustomed to Evergreen Hill. He still knew the town, despite having wanted to put it all behind him so many years ago. "I can't believe how little has changed," he said, turning his attention back to Samuel. He was startled to find that Samuel was looking at him intently, his brow furrowed as though he was thinking about something important. "What?"

"I'm just… you're a lot different than what I was expecting you to grow into," he said, a thoughtfulness to his words that caught Rory off guard. "I had all these ideas about what kind of man you would be if we ever met again."

"*I'm* different?" Rory asked, raising his eyebrows in surprise. "Have you looked in a mirror?"

"Really?" Samuel asked, widening his eyes in return, a longtime habit of mocking Rory when he made a look of surprise. Rory kicked him lightly under the table, and Samuel laughed, shaking his head. "How am I different? I feel like I'm pretty much the same."

"When I left, you were talking nonstop about being the next Kurt Cobain," Rory said. "Now you're running a lodge and, from what I've heard, you're a pastry chef. Not to mention you're way taller than you were before."

"And more handsome," Samuel added, Rory rolling his eyes in response. They had settled back into the easy friendship that had defined their relationship since they were children, and Rory wondered if it was emblematic of how Evergreen Hill made him feel as a whole: like he was no different at his core, just a confused teenager running away from his home and toward the unknown. "I can still play the guitar, if that's what you're worried about."

"Let me guess, you bust it out when there's carols to be sung, right?"

"Okay, unfair but accurate," Samuel said. "I might have changed, but you're the one who—" He was interrupted from saying more when the barista called out his name, and he quickly hopped to his feet, tapping his knuckles against the table. "Hold that thought."

Rory watched him walk over to the counter, resting his elbow against the table and his chin on his hand. Filled with an implacable feeling—longing, perhaps?—he found he couldn't take his eyes off the man. He drank in the sight of Samuel from behind, his hair curling over the collar of his flannel, his shoulders broad and defined, his waist tapered. Honestly, the man had gone from being built like a toothpick to like a Dorito, and Rory couldn't get over it. He hated himself in that moment, his attraction to Samuel as white-hot then as it had been when he'd left. Now, though, Samuel was married, a father, and Rory knew he had no place in his life.

"What are you staring at?"

Rory looked up to find that Malcolm and Ty had materialized, both of them flushed from the chill weather outside. To Rory's immense surprise, Malcolm was carrying Ty's bag for him, a gesture that was totally contrary to the selfishness Rory had come to expect from his coworker. He was also kind of smiling, a softness to the corners of his eyes that made his entire face look gentler. "What are you doing here?"

"Slide over," Malcolm instructed. Rory did as he was told, and Malcolm slipped into the booth alongside him. Ty settled across from him where Samuel had been, and Rory realized they both had drinks, albeit in to-go cups, and not the mugs used for sit-in diners. "Have you met Ty yet?"

"Not yet," Rory said, sticking his hand out. Ty shook it, his grip firm, and Rory was seized by guilt. His lie at the beginning of their trip had not only turned his relationship with Samuel on its head but had stopped Malcolm from being able to pursue Ty the way he wanted. "Although... did we meet at that gala last year?"

"I think we had a short conversation," Ty said, but he seemed just as foggy on the details. "I saw your interview in the *Architecture Times*, though. It was really eye-opening. You're very talented."

"So are you," Rory said. "Your editorial photographs are really some of the best I've ever seen. Malcolm said you're in town scouting for a Christmas movie?"

"Yeah, it's actually been really good," Ty said, eyes lighting up. "I guess Malcolm had done a lot of research on the town before you guys came, and he's been showing me all these little spots that are really great to photograph. We were taking pictures across the street when we saw you."

Samuel reappeared, balancing both the coffee and a plate of pastries, and seemed mildly surprised to see Ty and Malcolm. "Visitors!" he exclaimed, setting the coffees down and making sure Rory had his americano before sliding into the booth next to Ty. Rory didn't miss the look Samuel gave Malcolm, but to his continued surprise, he found that Malcolm met Samuel's gaze and nodded to him almost politely. Had he missed some turning point while he'd been holed up in his room? "Were you guys following us?"

"Other way around," Ty said. "Who runs the hotel when you're not there? Jasper?"

Samuel laughed, sounding genuinely caught off guard by the idea of his son running the lodge. "No way. He's responsible, but not that responsible. He figured out when he was a kid how to cry on command, so whenever an issue comes up, he just pretends to cry before coming to get me. Clark and Juliet are in charge right now."

Rory swallowed the bite of croissant he had taken, his eyes darting to Samuel at the mention of Juliet and another man. Samuel seemed totally relaxed, however, and a moment later Malcolm rested his hand on Rory's thigh under the table, as though warning him. Rory realized he was being way too obvious and coached himself into relaxing, scanning Samuel carefully. "Who's Clark?"

"You remember Clark," Samuel said, and when Rory looked at him with no comprehension, Samuel leaned forward a bit. "He was two years ahead of us at school. Huge guy, linebacker on the football team. His dad owned the hardware store?"

A memory came to Rory, a blond guy, well over six feet tall and built like a brick house manning the cash register at the hardware store whenever he and Samuel would pick up stuff for his parents' B&B. "He works at the lodge?"

"He's the head chef," Samuel said. "It worked out really nicely, because I can match his and Juliet's schedules so their kids are taken care of."

Malcolm's fingers dug into Rory's thigh, and Rory realized that his coworker knew him better than he had anticipated and had undoubtedly realized that Rory had misinterpreted the entire situation. Despite the warning, Rory couldn't help but laugh, a strange relief flooding him at the knowledge that Samuel wasn't married to Juliet. He was beginning to suspect that Samuel wasn't married at all, but the giddiness of that realization was quickly replaced by the fact that Rory had fucked himself over before he had even discerned the truth. "Juliet's not your wife?"

Samuel looked genuinely stunned, his fingers flexing against the mug in his hands. "Of course not," he said. "Why did you think that?"

"Well, because she works with you and—" Rory was quiet for a moment, brow furrowed as he realized he didn't have any other reason. "Oh my God."

"You're an idiot," Malcolm said, sighing softly and removing his hand from Rory's thigh since his warning had clearly been ignored. "Did you really look at none of the research for the lodge before we got here?"

"I looked at the blueprints, not the personnel," Rory said, looking at Samuel. "You're not married?"

"No," Samuel said, shaking his head. "No, I'm not. Why did you think I was?"

"Your ring," Rory said, and now that his amusement at his mistake was fading, he was realizing exactly what a terrible mistake it had been. He had panicked on his first day back, had seen the ring and Jasper, and had preemptively closed himself off in anticipation of being told that the man he had once loved desperately now loved someone else. "You have a wedding ring on."

Samuel looked at his left hand and the plain gold ring that sat there, a frown tugging at his lips. "I wear this so people don't hit on me," he admitted. "I swear, if I was married you would have met them by now."

Them. Not her, *them.* Rory was the biggest idiot who had ever existed, but before he could really allow that to sink in, Malcolm was holding him by the bicep. "I need to have a word with my fiancé," he said, dragging Rory out of the booth and toward the bookstore. They stopped in a small nook, Malcolm frowning down at Rory intently. "You need to come clean," he said, his voice low. "Just tell him you overreacted when you saw the ring on his finger."

"I can't admit that to him," Rory hissed, anxiety creeping up his spine as he thought of how Samuel would react to his choice. Rather than attempt to confront his feelings, he had lied, had forced Malcolm into his lie, and then had continued to distance himself from Samuel in the meantime. "Do you have any idea how psycho he'll think I am?"

"He knows you," Malcolm murmured. "He won't think it's psycho, he'll just think it's normal for you."

"Thanks," Rory said, rolling his eyes. "But it's not normal, even for me. I just acted without thinking, and I can't fucking admit it to him. He'll never speak to me again."

"You already weren't speaking," Malcolm said. "Besides, Ty already knows."

A sudden chill went through Rory, his eyes going wide. "You told him?"

"He point-blank asked me this morning if I was planning on cheating on you with him. I don't want him to think I'm some kind of monster, so I told him the truth."

"What did he say?"

"That you're an idiot and that you should tell Samuel the truth," Malcolm said, pinching the bridge of his nose as though he was another stupid question away from losing his mind. "I really don't want to keep this up until Christmas, but I also don't want to be the one to tell him because I think it would jeopardize our work here. You need to be the one to tell him, Rory. I mean it."

It was good advice, but admitting to Samuel that he had lied simply to avoid dredging up old feelings was a sort of humiliation he didn't think he could bear. "Did you kiss him?"

"Samuel?" Malcolm asked, face wrinkling in disgust. Rory stared at him before Malcolm cottoned on, cheeks turning pink, to Rory's immense surprise. "No. No, not yet. I'm going to, though."

"You know if I come clean our deal for the partnership is off."

"I'm aware. I'll beat you the old-fashioned way and impress Ty even more." He looked past Rory, who turned to see what he was looking at and found Ty standing with his camera in hand. "We're going to visit the candy store and see if they'll allow us to photograph the candy-cane-making process."

"I legitimately can't believe I'm hearing you say that," Rory said, entirely awestruck. "You're going where to do what?"

"Fuck off," Malcolm said, but Rory could hear the slight amusement in his voice even as the man walked past him to meet up with Ty. Rory waited for a minute before walking back to the booth and sliding in across from Samuel, who was politely pretending to be distracted by something on his phone.

"Sorry," Rory said, taking a sip of his now-lukewarm coffee. "He was trying to get me to not embarrass myself."

"No problem," Samuel said, but Rory could hear a strange note in his voice, a strained quality that hadn't been there before. "I think it's about time we head back to the lodge, yeah?"

"Oh, sure," Rory said, disappointment creeping over him. He'd been having such a nice morning with Samuel, but it had just been a distraction from the fact that Rory had irreparably damaged their relationship, both by leaving and now by lying. "Let's go."

Chapter Ten

"Done!" Jasper hopped off the last rung of the ladder and turned to survey their handiwork, the massive tree lit from bottom to top and ready for decorations. Louis turned to look with him, whistling softly at the sight, and Jasper grinned. "Looks good, doesn't it? There's a reason they call me the master of light stringing."

"I don't think anyone in human history has been called that," Louis said, laughing. "But you did a good job."

"So did you, ladder holder," Jasper said. "Time for your reward." He turned to look at the other teen, eyes bright. If he was being honest with himself, spending the morning with Louis had done wonders for his mood. He'd been upset on his father's behalf the day prior, worried that Rory's reappearance was going to do more harm than good, but that had all faded into the background, replaced by Louis's conversation and willingness to spend the morning on something that Jasper usually did with nothing but Spotify for company. "Go get your winter gear while I put the ladder away. I wanna take you somewhere."

"Okay, as long as you swear you won't murder me in the woods," Louis said, but he was still laughing as he headed to the elevator. Jasper waited until the doors closed behind him before turning and running to the kitchen at full speed. He burst through the doors, Juliet and Clark looking up from where they were working on the mise en place for that night's dinner, and threw his hands in the air.

"I need help," he said, trying not to panic. "I've convinced Louis to go up the mountain with me to the lookout my dad made when I was a kid, but I need you guys to help me. I have to go get changed really quick. Clark, can you put the ladder away? Jules, will you *please* pour a thermos of hot chocolate? I'm so stupid, I didn't think he'd actually say yes!"

"Okay, calm down," Clark said, setting down his knife and stepping around the counter. "Go get dressed. We'll put your date together for you."

"It's not a date," Jasper said, but as soon as he said it, a blush crept up his neck and cheeks. "Oh my God. Is it? Why did you say that!" He didn't stick around to get an answer, racing down the hallway that took him to the quarters where he and his father lived and missing the look that Clark and Juliet had given one another. Years of working for Samuel had made them entirely accustomed to the personalities of both men.

Jasper used his doorframe to propel himself into his bedroom, taking the corner so quickly that he nearly wiped out before barely managing to catch himself. His room was cozy and decorated with various art pieces he'd done over the years, along with pictures he'd taken, including a corkboard pinned with snapshots of him and his father. It was also surprisingly neat, and if Jasper had made sure it was clean just in case he and Louis needed somewhere to hang out, he would never admit it.

Jasper changed out of his T-shirt into a heavier sweater and found a scarf his grandmother had made him and his winter gear. His boots were by the back door of the living quarters, and he shoved them on, laced them up faster than he'd ever done in the past, and made sure he was fully weather ready by stealing one of his father's beanies. He had calmed down somewhat when he returned to the kitchen, where Juliet gave him a raised-eyebrow look. "You know you can plan ahead for dates, right?"

"I'm sorry, I'm sorry," Jasper said, squeezing her into a tight hug. "I just wasn't expecting this to happen today. I promise I'll make it up to you and Clark. Free babysitting for a month."

"You already babysit for free, you drama queen," Juliet said, but she hugged him back before letting go and turning back to the prep counter. She picked up an insulated backpack that they usually put together for guest excursions and held it out to him, Jasper's eyes going large at the sight of it. "There's hot chocolate, sandwiches, and some scones," she said by way of explanation. "Make sure you guys are back by dinner, and keep an eye on the clouds because there's snow in the forecast."

"Thanks, Mom," Jasper teased, hauling the backpack over his shoulder and looking up when Clark entered the kitchen. "Is he back?"

"Not yet," Clark said, shaking his head. "I'd get a move on, through."

"Thank you," Jasper said, hugging Clark quickly as well before dashing back out into the lobby. He nodded to the worker at the front desk, trying to get himself under control as he waited for Louis to reappear. Luckily he didn't have long to wait at all, as the elevator door opened and Louis emerged. He was dressed impeccably in ski pants and a windbreaker, his dark hair hidden under a knit hat, and he beamed at Jasper when he saw him, the simple action sending a lance of desire through Jasper's heart.

"All right," he said once he was within earshot, sticking his hands in the pockets of his coat and looking at Jasper. "Where are you taking me?"

"You'll see," Jasper said. "First we have to take the ski lift."

"Got it," Louis said, nodding resolutely. "Ski lift."

His dad had gone all out when he'd bought the lodge, renovating it from a dated 1970s eyesore to a modern and sleek venture, and that extended to the ski area. An outdoor bar butted up against the ski rental shop, the ski lift just beyond it and relatively busy. Despite the lull at the lodge itself, there were plenty of people who came just to ski. "Do we need skis?" Louis asked, looking over at the rental shop. "I'm not very good."

Unbidden, a rom-com movie scene of Jasper teaching Louis how to ski sprang to mind. Jasper shook it off, hoping that Louis would think his resulting blush was due to the cold, and grinned at him. "No, don't worry, I won't make you go skiing today. I just want to show you something. Uh, payment for holding the ladder."

"Wow, so generous," Louis said, laughing, and Jasper was struck by a sudden pang of adoration. He had never met someone so quick to laugh at his stupid jokes, and it was only serving to deepen his crush. "Have you lived at the lodge your whole life?"

"My dad bought it when I was like… seven, I think," Jasper said. He led Louis over to the ski lift, pausing to greet the girl manning it before grabbing Louis's hand to ensure they could get a chair together. They hopped on, Jasper's heart thrumming as Louis didn't immediately withdraw his hand. Despite the fact that they were both wearing gloves, Jasper could feel the heat of the other man's hand through the fabric, and when he finally mustered up the nerve to let go, he couldn't help but fixate on the lingering sensation. "We lived with my grandparents before that, but the lodge is really the only home I've ever known, since my dad was working here before he bought it. Have you guys always lived in New York?"

"No, we were in London when I was born, and then Dubai for a while," Louis said, shaking his head and peering up at the mountain as the chair continued its ascent. "We moved back when I was in sixth grade. I'm planning on staying in New York for school, though. I got accepted to NYU on early decision."

Jasper's face lit up, a thrill going through him. "Seriously?" he asked, gripping the arm of the ski lift so he could turn to look at Louis a little better. "NYU is my top pick. I got early acceptance as well, but… well, I haven't told my dad yet."

"That is so fucking cool," Louis said, and he looked entirely sincere as he said it. "We could be roommates, if you wanted. Not that you need to decide right now. I just think you'd be so easy to live with."

Another unbidden scene of the pair of them hit Jasper, this time in a cozy apartment together, baking on a snowy day and clearly just enjoying each other's company. Jasper was saved from sinking too far into the daydream by the lift reaching the top of the ski slope. He grabbed Louis's hand again and hopped off into the snow. "It's this way," he said, tugging Louis up the slope behind the ski lift enclosure. It wasn't that far of a hike, his dad having made it when Jasper was still quite a bit younger and not as good off-trail as he was now, and after five or so minutes of climbing through the snow, they reached their destination.

A huge oak tree sat on the edge of a clearing, a structure built among its boughs, and Jasper grinned at Louis. "Is this cheesy? It's my treehouse from when I was a kid. I used to spend literally all my time here."

"I don't think it's cheesy," Louis said. "I've… never been in a treehouse."

"Oh yeah, I guess you wouldn't have been," Jasper said. "Come on. The ladder's here. Go up first so I can catch you if you fall."

"Chivalrous," Louis said, but he clambered up the ladder easily, the treehouse less a fully formed building than it was a platform with a sloped roof to keep the snow out. As soon as Louis was up the ladder, Jasper climbed up after him, shrugged his backpack off, and set it between his legs. From the treehouse, the entirety of the mountain was visible: the ski lift, the lodge, the town beyond. It all looked like a dollhouse, beautiful and picturesque, and Jasper stole a look at Louis to see if he was impressed.

Instead, he found that Louis was looking at him. Jasper turned pink again, busying himself with unzipping his backpack and pulling out the lunch that Juliet had packed. He handed Louis a sandwich wrapped in wax paper, a blueberry scone, and poured a cup of hot chocolate into one of the mugs that screwed onto the top of the thermos. "You really came prepared," Louis said, and Jasper wasn't sure if he was reading into it or not, but he almost thought that the other teen had scooted closer to him. "Did you plan this earlier?"

"No, I got lucky that Juliet had my back when I decided to bring you up here," Jasper said. "I asked her to make us hot chocolate, and she went way above and beyond."

"That's really cute," Louis said as he unwrapped his sandwich and took a bite, looking out at the vista. "You guys are all, like, a little family, huh?"

"Well, my mom died when I was a baby," he said, shrugging. "It's always just been me and my dad and whoever he loves. Juliet and Clark really held him up when I was a kid, so I got them as a support system too."

"What's the story with your dad and Rory, anyway?" Louis asked. "I mean… I'm sorry, but the amount of time that blond guy is spending with the photographer? It's suspicious as hell. And neither of them have an engagement ring." Rory and Malcolm had been a topic of conversation between Jasper and Louis, particularly because Louis had recognized Malcolm as an infrequent attendant of parties his father threw, and trying to puzzle out the, frankly, soap opera-esque relationship between the adults was guaranteed conversation for hours. "Do you think they're actually engaged?"

"No, but like… why would Rory lie about that?" Jasper asked around a mouthful of sandwich. It had been eating him up inside, the idea that Rory had straight-up lied about being engaged for some unknown purpose, and he kept coming back to the same idea again and again: that he had done it solely to hurt Samuel. Every time he had that thought, though, he recalled the way that Rory looked at his father and was immediately ashamed that he doubted him to begin with. "Maybe it's some, like, BDSM thing."

Louis laughed so hard he nearly choked, covering his face with his hands before peeking at Jasper. "What are you even talking about?" he asked, the wind having disheveled his dark hair and caused it to fall over his forehead. Jasper was once again struck by how adorable he was. "Do you really think that?"

"No, of course not, it was totally a joke," Jasper said, laughing in return. He finished off his sandwich and became aware that Louis was still looking at him, turning to face the other boy fully. "What's up? Do I have something on my face?"

He lifted his hand self-consciously, but before he could touch his face, Louis had caught him by the wrist. Jasper blinked, briefly surprised, but he had no time to ask what Louis was doing because the other boy had leaned in and kissed him. His mouth was surprisingly warm despite the cold air surrounding them, his lips soft and nicer than Jasper had even imagined. He was no stranger to kissing, a handful of ex-boy- and girlfriends in his past, and yet the jolt of excitement that went through him when Louis kissed him was entirely new.

His surprise didn't stop him from kissing back, his lips parting slightly to allow Louis to kiss him deeper, and before he really realized what had even happened, he was being pressed against one of the posts holding up the sloped roof. Louis drew back for a moment, searching his face for permission to keep going, and Jasper chased his mouth, kissing him again with fervor. Louis flexed his fingers against Jasper's wrist, his eyes closed as he leaned into Jasper more readily, and when they were forced to part once again to breathe, Louis laughed softly, resting his forehead against Jasper's. "Sorry," he murmured. "I've wanted to do that since day one."

"Me too," Jasper said, his face flushed and his heart racing so fast he thought his chest might burst. "I didn't, uh, I didn't realize you liked me like that."

"I didn't realize how much I did until I was looking at you just now," Louis said, dropping his head down to rest against Jasper's collarbone. He peered out at the mountain, Jasper hoping that Louis found the vista as breathtaking as Jasper always did. "I hope my dad keeps everything the same."

Jasper, still stunned by the kiss, barely registered what Louis had said, unable to tear his gaze away from the other boy. As soon as Louis kissed him again, anything he had said before that point was rendered moot, his natural curiosity overcome by his desire to have the other boy's lips on his.

Chapter Eleven

"ARE YOU speaking to me again?"

Rory lifted his head from where he was crouching next to their box of tree ornaments, narrowing his eyes in response, and Malcolm frowned down at him. "I haven't decided yet," Rory finally said, choosing a fat snowman from the selection and straightening up so he could hang it on a branch. "Why should I?"

Rory would readily admit he was in a bad mood, that he'd been in a bad mood since the day prior when his and Samuel's morning had been abruptly cut short. Rory had been able to tell that Samuel was upset, but beyond that he couldn't suss out anything further. They had driven back to the lodge together, had engaged in shallow but relatively pleasant conversation, and since then they hadn't spoken.

It was all made worse by the fact that today was the Christmas tree-decorating event and every guest in the place was gathered in the lobby. A tree was provided for each booked room—anyone who was coming later would be given one already in their suite—and the lobby was bustling. Rory and Malcolm were near the sitting area, the Caldwell's across the lobby. Even Juliet and Clark had been given the opportunity to decorate a tree, their children doing their best to hang all their ornaments in the exact same spot on the tree from the way it looked on Rory's end.

Rory looked down at the snowman in his hand, frowning at its fat little smiling face. Each tree was themed—gingerbread, silver and gold, every Christmas cliché—and he and Malcolm had been dealt snowmen. Rory understood why they'd done it in such a way, the themes allowing for identification of the trees and minimal overlap of ornaments, but he was too irritated and caught up in his own feelings that morning to enjoy the task at hand. He hung the snowman from one of the top branches and turned back to the ornament box, only to find Malcolm watching him with his arms crossed.

"Stop it," he said, his frown deepening. "You looking at me like that isn't helping me at all."

"Looking at you like what?" Malcolm asked. "However you're feeling when I'm looking at you has nothing to do with me. I'm just looking."

"You're *not* just looking," Rory grumbled, grabbing another ornament and nearly crushing it in his hand with how hard he gripped it. "You've got this dumb look in your eyes that's half pity and half irritation. Just say it."

"I already said it yesterday, and you got upset with me," Malcolm said, and if Rory was a more violent person, he would have kicked the other man in the shin for the tone he was using. "You need to tell Samuel the truth."

"Okay, I get it, but I can't do it right away," Rory said, the mere thought of fessing up to what he'd done sending waves of anxiety through him. "I need to think it over."

"What's to think over?" Malcolm asked, removing a garland that resembled a knit scarf from the ornament box and looking at it with clear dislike before slowly beginning to wrap it around the tree. "You lied to him, you pulled me into it, and now you're ruining my life."

"I'm not ruining your life, you fucking drama queen," Rory said. "How was I supposed to know that after a hundred business trips together this would be the one where you found the single person on the planet who actually likes you?"

"He does like me," Malcolm said, seemingly unbothered by Rory's condemnation. "And we had an excellent day yesterday. I've seen almost all the selling points in town to take back to the firm, and Ty has agreed to photograph our next year of grand openings. However, he's made it abundantly clear that he won't kiss me until Samuel knows that you and I aren't a thing. I think he still thinks I'm lying to him about the whole fake fiancé thing, which… I don't blame him, actually."

"I'm not trying to ruin your chances," Rory said. "I just… I need time to figure out how to word this to him. Like, I know how insane it sounds. But when I saw Samuel with a kid and a ring on his finger, all I could think was that I was still that heartbroken kid I was when I left, you know?"

"No," Malcolm said, looking at him as though he were insane. "No, Rory, how could I possibly know that? You know you've said almost nothing to me, right? Whatever you went through, I have no way of knowing what it was. All I really know is that you left for the city and Samuel didn't. Why are you so damn afraid of burning a bridge that already burned twenty years ago?"

Rory frowned, glancing toward the tree where Samuel and Jasper were working. He couldn't have known it, but Samuel had just looked away from him in turn. "Fine," he said. "But if you use any of this against me, I'll actually kill you."

"I highly doubt that," Malcolm said. "But tell me anyway."

Rory sighed, redoubling his attention to decorating so he didn't have to look at Malcolm while he spoke. "I was a seriously lonely kid. My parents weren't abusive or anything, they just weren't around all that often because of work. I still don't really talk to them much. When I started school, I met Samuel, and we were immediately best friends. Like, I can't think of a time when I felt more at home with a person. We started spending all our time together, every last second, and I didn't know it at the time, but I was already starting to fall in love with him. We didn't realize it until we were older, like fifteen or so, but once we did, we were even more inseparable. His parents went so far as to make me a spare room in their basement, and they helped get me a job on their friend's Christmas tree farm."

Rory paused, unsure why he was confiding so much in Malcolm when the two of them had been at odds throughout the entirety of their working relationship. If he had known that having Malcolm pretend to be his fiancé would be the key to thawing the ice between them, he would have done it earlier.

Well, no, he wouldn't have ever done this under any other circumstances, but Rory could feel a seed of friendship growing. Bizarre as this had all been, Malcolm was listening to him without judgment, although he was admittedly struggling with hanging the garland. When he realized that Rory had stopped talking, he looked over at him, quirking an eyebrow. "So you were in love," he prompted. "How does that turn into not seeing each other for twenty years?"

"I wasn't content," Rory said. "I always felt... inadequate. Like I wasn't doing all I could do. And Samuel... I loved him so much that all I wanted was to give him the best life I possibly could. I desperately wanted to prove myself. I was good at math, and I had always wanted to be an architect, ever since I was a kid and saw this coffee table book about the Chrysler Building. I thought if I was an architect, I could give him the life I thought he deserved. But I think I never realized that he didn't want that. He didn't want to live in the city and wait for me to finish school. He liked living here, and he liked working with his parents. I couldn't fathom it because I wanted such a different thing, and I just ended up bulldozing him into accepting a life I wanted."

"What happened when you left town?"

"He didn't show up for the bus," Rory said. "I figured, uh, that something had happened with his sister, but he didn't page me or anything." He laughed, shaking his head. "God, I never thought I'd be wishing I had a cellphone back then, but it could have cleared so much up. He just never arrived, and when I got to New York and called his house, no one answered. I thought that was it, that was his answer." He glanced over his shoulder, Samuel laughing with his kid, and felt such a strong pang of longing that he thought it might kill him. "But seeing him, talking to him… I don't know."

"What don't you know?" Malcolm asked, letting go of the garland and stepping back. It was crooked, but Rory knew his colleague well enough by now to recognize that he would have to be the one who fixed it. "It seems pretty clear to me that the guy still has intense feelings for you. He looks at you constantly, and you made him cry the other day."

"Then why didn't he even try to reach out?" Rory asked, deciding to let the crooked garland slide; it was more charming this way. "I don't understand why it had to end when it did."

"I think it's pretty obvious," Malcolm said. "The kid."

Rory's brow furrowed, and he shook his head, his expression grim. "I don't believe that."

"Why?"

"Because if the reason he didn't come to New York with me was Jasper, then that… that means he cheated on me," Rory said, the mere idea of Samuel having been unfaithful as teenagers totally impossible to fathom. "I don't think that he would have done that. There's absolutely no way he had sex with anyone else while we were dating."

"I'm not saying he cheated on you," Malcolm said, looking at Rory meaningfully. "Think about it. What would have stopped him from coming with you? What has he consistently shown as important to him?"

Rory considered this, crouching down to lift one of the last ornaments from the container. "His family," he hedged, before he realized what exactly Malcolm was getting at. "Oh my God. You think Jasper's not his kid?"

Malcolm shrugged, looking down at him. "Look, I'm not a psychic or anything, but it seems to me like the most obvious answer is that

Jasper's not his son. Or at least not biologically his son. If he had a reason to stay and you're sure he wouldn't have cheated on you with some girl, then it's clear something else happened."

Rory looked over at Samuel again, this time catching the other man looking at him in return. Their gazes met for a moment before Samuel tore his eyes away and turned back to his son. Something else? Come to think of it, Samuel had mentioned his parents frequently, but not his sister, Jamie. Had something happened to her that had prevented Samuel from following him? "You might have a point," he finally admitted, crossing his arms over his chest and realizing Malcolm had hit the nail on the head. Their entire childhood, Samuel had never expressed even a passing interest in women, and his parents had accepted his sexuality without batting an eye. Rory could still remember the conversation they'd had as a group, the elder Danielses making it abundantly clear that they couldn't ask for a better match for Samuel, and that didn't add up to Samuel immediately finding consolation with someone else, especially not a girl.

"I know I have a point," Malcolm said forcefully. "I might be an oblivious bastard, Rory, but I can see pretty clearly that Samuel is still in love with you."

That was a line too far, a proclamation that Rory simply couldn't accept. He peered up at the other man, internally cursing at the way his heart had pitched wildly as soon as he'd thought about Samuel holding a torch for him all this time. Had he always felt the same? Had he always thought that maybe one day he would end up in front of the other man again, albeit not with the idiotic baggage he had attached to himself? "There's no way," he said, shaking his head to rid himself of the thought. "I'm sorry, but there's no way a guy who looks like Samuel has just been waiting idly for me to come back."

"I'm not saying he's been celibate, moron. I'm saying he's seen you now and he's realized that he's one hundred percent still in love with you," Malcolm said, fishing the last ornament from the box, a star with a snowman's face on it, and leaning up to place it on the top of the tree. "It doesn't really matter how many guys he's fucked in the interim if he ends up with you at the end."

"Ugh, don't say that so casually," Rory said, feeling his face flush and immediately being thankful his skin was dark enough that Samuel wouldn't be able to see it at a distance. "I don't want to think about that."

"So you're still pining for him, and he's still pining for you," Malcolm said. "Seems obvious that you tell him the truth, doesn't it?"

"I don't believe he's pining for me," Rory said, stepping back to observe the tree and starting slightly when Malcolm took a step after him. "Why are you following me?"

"I figured you'd still have objections," he said. "And I made up my mind last night that I'm going to convince you to tell him the truth one way or another."

Rory furrowed his brow, looking up at Malcolm as an ominous chill jolted through him. "What does that mean?" he asked, but before he could say more or get an answer, Malcolm's mouth was on his. It was possibly the last thing on the planet Rory had expected.

Every inch of him fought against being kissed, and yet he managed to stop himself from looking overly tense, his saving grace the same quick thinking that had gotten him into this mess. This was clearly Malcolm's attempt to force him into admitting the fraud, gambling that Rory's disgust at being kissed would get him to rebel against the man he claimed was his fiancé, and Rory wouldn't give him the satisfaction. Malcolm's mouth was soft, inviting, tasted slightly of bergamot, and while Rory did not kiss back, he did not pull away either.

When Malcolm drew away, there was a smirk on his lips that made Rory have to fight not to step on his insole as hard as he possibly could. "Look at him," he said, and for a moment Rory was truly oblivious before he realized what Malcolm was saying and turned his head to look across the lobby at Samuel.

What he saw in the other man's eyes was a pain that nearly took his breath away. Samuel was staring at them, an ornament held loose in his hand, and Rory's lungs suddenly seemed incapable of holding air. As soon as Samuel realized Rory was looking at him he turned away, his broad shoulders tense, and Rory realized that by turning to look at him he had only reinforced the idea that he was rubbing Malcolm in his face. "Fuck," he whispered, looking up at Malcolm and ignoring the part of his brain telling him to flee. "Why'd you do that?"

"I told you why," Malcolm said. "I'm not above playing dirty to get what I want, and what I want right now is for you to tell Samuel the truth."

"You are so lucky I didn't just kick you in the nutsack," Rory sneered, any professionalism he'd been clinging to going out the window as his anger flared again. "You can't just kiss someone like that!"

"I didn't kiss someone like that, I kissed you," Malcolm said, and Rory was even more infuriated by his continued calm than he was by anything else. "And I'll do it again if you don't tell Samuel. I'm about to be a nightmare of public affection if you don't figure yourself out, do you understand?"

"You're a fucking pervert," Rory said, poking Malcolm hard in the chest. "Scottish pervert."

"For kissing my fiancé?" Malcolm asked, and Rory stifled the urge to punch him, wondering how the fuck he had been so stupid as to willingly enlist this man as his co-conspirator. "There's a simple solution to the problem, isn't there? Tell him."

"Okay, I get it," Rory said, his words little more than a hiss, and while he knew the choice should have been easy, the idea of admitting to Samuel what he had done was so anxiety-inducing it felt like eels squirming in his gut.

Chapter Twelve

THEIR TREE decorated and placed with the others along the wall, the lobby now jam-packed with Christmas cheer from floor to ceiling, Rory made his quick escape. He was too pissed at Malcolm to do much more than give him a dirty look before making a beeline upstairs, letting himself into their room, and trying to figure out what he could do to ensure that he didn't have to spend time with Malcolm for a little bit. He wanted time to think, time to really consider what he needed to do here, and Malcolm pressuring him into telling Samuel the truth wasn't exactly helping him take an unbiased viewpoint.

He gathered up his laptop and the rough blueprints he'd been working on, passed Malcolm on his way out the door, and paused only when the other man grabbed him by the arm. "What?" Rory asked, pulling away. "I'm mad at you."

"Don't be," Malcolm said. "Where are you going?"

"The bar to get some work done," Rory said, narrowing his eyes. "Don't follow me."

"I won't," Malcolm said. "But I can guarantee that I'll kiss you in front of Samuel again if you don't figure your shit out fast."

"You shouldn't have kissed me in the first place," Rory hissed, kicking Malcolm hard in the shin, and he was perfectly aware that even a week ago he never would have considered kicking Malcolm despite how poorly they got along. Was that indicative of a better relationship between them or a worse one? Rory had enough to think about without adding a possible friendship with Malcolm to the mix, and before the other man could say anything, he'd turned and practically fled down the hallway.

The bar, like the restaurant, was attached to the lodge but facing the ski resort so guests didn't have to cross through the hotel to reach it. Rory found an out-of-the-way booth that allowed him to spread his things out and ordered a glass of red wine, prepared to really hunker down and work. As simple as that sounded in theory, however, it was proving almost impossible in reality. His thoughts were consumed with what had happened earlier, less so with the fact that Malcolm had kissed him—an event that he would be entirely happy to never repeat again—and more so with the look on Samuel's face.

He didn't think he'd ever seen that kind of heartbreak in someone's eyes before, but it seemed entirely impossible to believe. It had been twenty years, twenty long fucking years, and even Rory had made some attempts to move on. Sure, he'd failed miserably, and sure, he'd never had a relationship that had lasted longer than a year or so, but he'd still tried. Had Samuel tried? Had he dated other people, only to come to the realization at the end that it wasn't what he wanted?

How the hell was he supposed to get any work done when he couldn't stop thinking about the twenty years apart, when he couldn't resolve the internal struggle between going to Samuel and staying exactly where he was?

"Why do you look like that?"

Rory started, looking up once he realized he was the person being spoken to and finding Ty standing at the end of the table, brow furrowed. "You scared me," Rory said, heaving a sigh. "What are you doing?"

"I was sitting over there working and saw you," Ty said, pointing to a two-seater across the bar that currently held a laptop and what looked like a mug of coffee. "Worked out nicely. I wanted to talk to you without Mal or Samuel around. Can I bring my stuff over?"

"Sure," Rory said, deciding not to comment on the nickname for Malcolm, the two of them proving themselves so sickly sweet in their flirtation that it was kind of insane. He watched as Ty returned to his table, gathering his things and chatting briefly with a waiter before coming back to Rory's booth and settling down across from him. "You really call him Mal?"

"He hates it," Ty said, grinning. "So yes. I was kind of surprised to see you here, honestly. I thought you guys were getting along better."

"Ugh," Rory said, looking at Ty intently. "I guess you weren't at the Christmas tree decorating."

"I don't celebrate," Ty said. "Although I really like eggnog. Does that count?"

"I don't think so," Rory said. "Malcolm kissed me."

If he had expected any jealousy on Ty's end—which, considering the personalities of both men involved, he really hadn't—he didn't get it.

Instead, Ty laughed so loudly that a man sitting nearby jumped in clear fear, turning his head to look at them both. Ty immediately covered his mouth with one hand, shaking his head as he tried to compose himself. "Of course he did," he said. "In front of Samuel?"

"Did you guys plan that?"

"No, but after we spent the day together yesterday, he tried to kiss me, and I told him I wasn't comfortable with it. Not because I think you two are actually together, but because I didn't want someone seeing us and getting the wrong idea. So he said he was going to make you break up with him. I guess he was serious."

Rory sighed, tilting his head back against the cushioned back of the booth and staring at the exposed beams of the ceiling. "I know that I'm being selfish right now, but I just… I don't know. I feel like the world's biggest idiot, honestly."

"Look, I know you're embarrassed that you jumped to conclusions like that, but do you really think Samuel won't forgive you? I just see no way that this doesn't become a cute story you tell to whatever kids Jasper has down the road."

"It's not…." Rory tried to organize his thoughts, realizing that as soon as he had agreed for Ty to join him he'd given up any ability to work. Most frustrating of all, he realized that he liked Ty, that he found him blunt and funny, that he was well-suited to Malcolm's strange arrogance. It only piled onto the guilt he was feeling about the whole situation: about leading Samuel on, about interrupting what could be a truly good match for Malcolm, about avoiding a relationship with Jasper, who he desperately wanted to know. "It's not simple," he said finally. "It's more than just being embarrassed that I lied to him."

"Then what is it?"

Rory shifted on the seat, drumming his fingers against the table as he figured out what to say. "When we were kids, I was the impulsive one," he finally said. "I was constantly doing stuff without thinking, and Samuel always had to clean up after me. I just seemed incapable of keeping my mouth shut. When we were little, it wasn't as big of a deal. No one expects a seven-year-old to have great impulse control. But when we got to be teenagers, I had this huge chip on my shoulder. I was constantly picking fights or just pushing shit to the worst possible outcome. I couldn't help it, not really, but Samuel was always there to pull me out of whatever trouble I'd gotten myself into."

He paused, rubbing at his jaw before he took a sip of his wine just to wet his lips. "The summer before I left, Samuel and I drove down to Albany to go to this metal concert. We'd done it a hundred times by then, and we usually didn't do anything too crazy. I think the most trouble we'd ever gotten in was we got too drunk and had to sleep in a Walmart parking lot, but that last time we went down, I don't really know what happened. We were at the concert, and Samuel left me alone to go smoke. I was just hanging out waiting for him to come back, and this guy started hassling me. A Black guy in the nineties metal scene wasn't exactly rare, but it wasn't exactly the most usual thing, either, and this dude really thought I was infringing on some whites-only space."

"So you told him off?" Ty asked, raising a hand for the waiter. The man came over, refreshed his coffee, and left again. "Why would that make Samuel not forgive you for lying this time?"

"I didn't tell the guy off," Rory said. "I egged him on. I made the whole thing worse, both because he was pissing me off and because I hated the idea that someone thought I wasn't a metalhead just because I was Black. I wasn't even eighteen yet, this scrawny little thing, and the dude bothering me had to have been in his late twenties. I was ready to fight him, though, and I know things would have gone so bad if I'd had the chance. Samuel stopped me, though. He came back from smoking, found this racist idiot trying to fight me and me trying to fight him back, and in the middle of this crowd of people he asked the guy why he was hitting on a minor."

Ty grinned, raising his eyebrows. "I'm assuming your new friend didn't like that."

"No, he was pissed. But Samuel just got louder, and people started to pay attention. Eventually the show started, and the guy stayed the hell away from us, and Samuel held my hand the whole time like he thought I might try and pick another fight if he let me out of his sight. I couldn't stop thinking about it, though. How once again I'd made a situation worse, and how once again I'd been saved by Samuel. It was the first time I'd really recognized how detrimental my impulsiveness was to him, and I resolved to fix it. I didn't have time to demonstrate it, though, because just a couple months later we were separated."

Ty considered this, his own work clearly set aside for the moment as he allowed what Rory had said to sink in. "So you're telling me that after you decided to not be impulsive around Samuel anymore, the first thing you did after twenty years apart was pretend that Malcolm was your fiancé?"

Rory groaned, the bluntness of the situation really sinking in now that he had it confirmed by someone else. "Yeah, exactly. For twenty years, I recognized that I was impulsive and quick-tempered, and I worked so hard on that part of myself. At first it was because... well, because Samuel hadn't come with me, so clearly that meant there was something wrong with me to begin with. That was my biggest flaw, so it made sense to fix it. But after a while, it just became for me. Life was easier when I wasn't picking fights or jumping headfirst into stupid stunts. I chilled out, and I fixed that part of me that had caused so much trouble when I was younger. But the minute I got back here, it was like all of that hard work had just disappeared. I didn't even stop to think."

Ty looked at him, steepling his fingers together and resting his chin on them, pushing his lips into a pout. "Did Samuel ever complain?"

Rory frowned, his brow furrowing in confusion. "Complain?"

"About your being impulsive," Ty said. "Did he ever say he didn't like it or anything like that?"

Rory was quiet, finishing off his glass of wine and not stopping the waiter from topping it back up from the same bottle. The answer was, of course, no. Samuel had never complained about swooping in and saving Rory from his own recklessness. Even the night in question, where they easily could have fallen victim to violence thanks to Rory's inability to keep his mouth shut, had turned out fine. Samuel had found the whole thing funny and had recounted the story to his parents when they'd gotten back to Evergreen Hill the next day. He had held Rory's hand under the table and had laughed about the look on the guy's face.

Rory had done stupid stuff throughout his teenage years—throwing himself headlong off cliffs into far-off ponds, using a metal trashcan lid as a makeshift sled that ended with him nearly concussed against a fir tree—and yet Samuel had never turned away. He had never ignored what Rory did, had never asked him to change, had never even hinted he didn't like it or felt Rory was putting them at risk. "Jesus Christ," he mumbled, and Ty grinned.

"You're really dumb, huh?" he asked, raising his eyebrows. "I hope you're a better architect than you are a romantic."

"How did you figure this out so quickly?" Rory asked, jabbing a finger in the air toward Ty. "It's not like you know me."

"No, but you and Malcolm left me at the booth with Samuel when we were in town, remember?" Ty shrugged, his almond-shaped eyes creasing with clear amusement. "So there's me, trying to keep up the conversation, and there's him, staring daggers at Malcolm from across the cafe, and he straight-up says that he doesn't understand how a guy who once thought it was a cool idea to hang on to the back of a truck on a skateboard like Marty McFly could end up falling in love with someone who has literally no sense of humor. And the way he said it, it wasn't like… well, like he was upset about the skateboard thing, but that he was upset that you were no longer the kind of guy who would do something like that. Like he liked it when you guys were young and dumb."

"Are you making this up so you can have Malcolm free and clear?" Rory asked, narrowing his eyes in suspicion, and Ty grinned. "Ty, seriously."

"I'm not making it up, I swear," Ty said. "I mean, yes, I do want to make out with Malcolm and have a romantic Christmas, even though I don't celebrate and he's obviously a Scrooge, but do you know how romantic it would be for you and Samuel to reconcile? Just think about it. The single father and his childhood love?"

Rory rubbed at his forehead, a headache starting to prick behind his eyes. "Fine," he said finally, worn down by the day and by the look in Samuel's eyes when he'd been kissed. "Fine, I'll talk to him, but if this goes poorly, I'm actually going to kill you and Malcolm."

"Hey, that's pretty romantic," Ty said, getting to his feet. "Let's go."

"Let's go?" Rory repeated, staying where he was. "Go where?"

"To talk to Samuel," Ty said, waving down the waiter, who was looking increasingly like he didn't want to have any part of this, most likely because Rory and Ty were clearly talking about his employer. "Can you watch our things? I'll give you forty dollars."

"Fine," the waiter said, holding out his hand, and Ty dug through his pockets before finding his wallet and pressing some cash into the man's hand.

"Let's go," Ty repeated, and for some reason that Rory could not even fathom, he obediently got to his feet, nodded at the waiter, and followed Ty out of the bar. By that point he was so tired of all the blatant chicanery that he was ready to just tell the truth, but as soon as they entered the lobby it was clear that the truth would have to wait.

Samuel was standing at the check-in desk, Connor Caldwell across from him, and in between them on the counter was a thick packet of papers. Samuel's face was pale as a ghost, his hazel eyes wide, and as Ty and Rory approached it became clear that Connor Caldwell was smiling like a cat who'd just pinned a mouse under its paw. "What's going on?" Rory asked, foreboding creeping up the base of his skull, and Samuel looked at him, clearly stricken.

"I've just been served an injunction to close the lodge," Samuel said, swallowing hard. "Everything needs to be shut down by New Year's Day."

Chapter Thirteen

"OKAY, YOU know the rules," Samuel said, unhooking the keys to his truck from the lanyard he kept on his belt loop. He dangled them in front of Jasper, raising his eyebrows. "Say it."

Jasper rolled his eyes but without any actual irritation, shooting Louis a look that said this was typical. "I won't drive the truck off a cliff," he recited. "I won't drive into a gas station, I won't drink and drive, I won't run away to Canada to smuggle drugs." He grinned, reaching out to pluck the keys from his father's hand. "What if I just did all of that anyway?"

"If I thought you would, I wouldn't give you the keys," Samuel said, laughing. He reached out to ruffle Jasper's hair, taking care not to actually mess it up, and then gently pushed him toward Louis. "Have a good evening, okay? Don't go crazy with my card."

"Got it," Jasper said, turning to look at Louis. "You ready?"

With that, the two boys left, Samuel watching them with a growing sense of déjà vu. With the Christmas tree decorating over, he had been left to deal with his own emotions after seeing Rory kiss Malcolm. Hashing it out wasn't even an option since Rory had disappeared the second the trees had been finished, and Samuel had agreed to allow Jasper the evening off for a date. Trapped at the front desk, he was really only capable of wallowing in his feelings.

He couldn't count how many times he and Rory had begged Samuel's dad for the keys to his car in the years before they'd saved up enough for Samuel to buy a used pickup. As soon as his thoughts turned to Rory, however, a black hole opened up in his stomach. He wondered how fucked up it was that even when Rory had introduced Malcolm as his fiancé, Samuel had still held out some hope that there was a future for them.

Truthfully, he had never moved on. He had gone on a handful of dates here and there, had done his best to try and keep up with romance outside of what he'd lost when Rory had left, but he never stopped being that teenage boy who had cried his eyes out on his parents' sofa rather than catching the bus with the only person he'd ever loved. He knew it was a romantic fantasy out of some movie, but he had always assumed that he and Rory would find their ways back to one another at some point. He had never in a million years anticipated that reuniting would involve such a clear obstacle.

However, his hope had honestly still held out. He'd seen the way that Malcolm and Ty interacted with one another over the past week, and the vibe he'd gotten was that there was something going on there. If Malcolm was cheating, Rory would recognize it, but even after running into Malcolm and Ty on what was a clear date the day before Rory had seemed unperturbed. And today... today, the kiss. Samuel had seen Rory afterward, had seen the way that Rory looked at him, as though drawing his attention to what had happened, and the idea of Rory *gloating* that he had found someone else was really ruining his day.

He sighed, smoothing down the calendar he left on the front desk to keep the events straight and beginning to puzzle over the Christmas Eve schedule. Deciding to have the visit with Santa before the Christmas movie screening had worked in the past, but even trying to figure out something he did literally every year was proving difficult thanks to Rory haunting his thoughts. Samuel was so caught up in his own mind that he didn't hear footsteps on the floor of the lobby until a shadow fell across his calendar and he looked up to find Connor Caldwell standing in front of him.

He had to admit that the man had an air about him that was both intimidating and charming. Samuel had no idea what Connor did for a living, except that he was extremely successful. The cost to spend weeks at the lodge over Christmas was evidence enough, but the designer clothes Louis consistently sported were an additional hint. "Oh, hi," Samuel said, straightening up. "The boys just left. I gave Jasper the whole safe-driving spiel."

"Oh, don't worry, I trust your son," Connor said, smiling at Samuel. His teeth were blindingly white and impossibly straight, and Samuel briefly wondered whether they were real. "I actually wanted to talk with you."

"With me?" Samuel repeated. "Is everything okay with your room?"

"Oh, yes," Connor said. "We're having an excellent time. Honestly, it's impressive how thoughtful everything is. I can see why the lodge is so popular, especially at this time of year. You really put your whole heart into it."

There was something about the way that Connor was speaking, something in the way his blue eyes met Samuel's, that made his spine crawl with dread. "I try," Samuel said, still plastering on his customer service smile despite the authenticity of it flagging somewhat. "If everything is all right, then what's the matter?"

"Do you remember being approached by a holding company several years ago?" Connor asked, hoisting the cross-body satchel he'd been carrying up and opening the flap to remove a document bound with plastic spiral rings. "I believe it was a very fair offer to purchase the lodge."

"I remember," Samuel said, a chill descending on him. "I refused because the proposal was to tear down the lodge to make room for timeshares. That was your company?"

"One of them," Connor said. He had set the document on the desk, and Samuel looked at it, suddenly panged with anxiety. *Proposal to Replace the Evergreen Lodge with Timeshares* read the front page of the document, no different than it had been three years ago, and Samuel frowned, wondering why Connor thought his answer would be any different this time. "That's your copy, by the way."

"I appreciate the offer, but like before, I'm going to have to pass," Samuel said, putting his hand on top of the document and pushing it back toward Connor. "I'm not opposed to selling the lodge, but I won't do it if the building will be torn down."

"You haven't heard my pitch yet," Connor said, and there was that sinking feeling again. Samuel looked at him, waiting for him to continue, and Connor did just that. "Are you aware that the land to the south of your lodge was for sale?"

"The salt mine?" Samuel asked. "Yeah, I know. But that's all protected land. No development is allowed on it. I was looking at acquiring it myself to expand the ski resort before I learned that."

"You've done your research," Connor said, and Samuel was no longer finding his tone even remotely friendly; instead, he was pretty sure he was being condescended to. "After you turned down my first proposal, I did my research too." He opened the document and flipped through it to the middle. A pair of survey maps were there, the one on the left marked 1900 and the one on the right 1910. "Your lodge was built in 1897, correct?"

"Correct."

"In 1900, the property line for the salt mine encroached one hundred and forty feet over the edge of the current understood property line, covering an area equivalent to… oh, say, half of your current guest suites." He tapped the first map to illustrate. "And then in 1910, it looks as though the property line was moved to account for that land, no doubt due to a verbal agreement between the mine owner and the lodge owner at the time. However, in doing my research, I discovered that there were no legal documents filed."

Samuel's stomach sank. "The lodge has stood without issue for over a hundred years."

"Due to a verbal agreement between the mine owner and the lodge owner," Connor repeated. "But now I'm the mine owner, and I no longer think the agreement is all that fair. And since neither man thought it was necessary to file any actual documentation, the property line that existed in 1900 is the last *legal* property line. Meaning that as soon as the sale was finalized last month, I *legally* own one hundred and forty feet of your lodge."

Samuel was dumbstruck, his eyes fixated on the document on the front desk. He honestly couldn't remember the last time he felt this sick, an anxious sort of nausea creeping over him like a fog. "What does that mean?" he asked, and he was surprised at how stupid he sounded, how entirely unprepared. "I can't move the lodge, so…."

"No, you can't," Connor said. "Don't worry, the process is simple. I'm giving you until January first to close the lodge and until January fifteenth to move everything from the premises. The ski resort is still yours, unfortunately, but you and I should be able to come to a fair price on the sale of that."

"I'm not closing the lodge," Samuel said, indignant in his protest. "This can't be legal for you to do. You can't just swoop in here and tell me that you suddenly own half of my building."

"I don't," Connor agreed. "I own the land it sits on. I've already had an injunction prepared making the terms clear. The lodge closed and emptied." He flipped further into the documentation, tapping on a page that Samuel read over. It was a clear injunction from a local judge informing Samuel that he needed to cease operation of the lodge until the property line dispute could be properly investigated and settled. The entire thing seemed straightforward, solid, and that made it a hundred times worse. He was still trying to wrap his mind around it when he became aware of other people approaching the desk.

Looking up, he found Rory standing there, Ty Choi following close behind. The moment his eyes met Rory's, an awful selfish thought struck him and he had to fight to force it back down. "What's going on?" Rory asked, brow furrowed in concern, and Samuel shook his head.

"I've just been served an injunction to close the lodge," he said, his mouth dry. "Everything needs to be shut down by New Year's Day."

"What?" Rory and Ty asked in unison, and Connor grinned.

"I'll leave you now," he said, closing the documentation and pushing it toward Samuel once again. He stepped past the pair on his way to the elevator, Rory watching him go before walking over to the desk and reaching out to put his hand on the paperwork. Before Samuel even realized what he was doing, he had reached out in return to block him, and surprise crossed Rory's face.

"Sorry," Rory said, looking confused but dropping his hand back to his side nonetheless. "You were being serious? How the hell is that even legal?"

"He bought the old salt mine, and the land boundary was never legally updated," Samuel said quietly. "Because the lodge is on the land in question, it has to close for the investigation to happen." He paused, not wanting to suspect it but also unable to ignore the growing suspicion he had. "Did you know about this?"

Rory stared at him as though he hadn't heard him correctly. "Sorry?"

"It just makes no sense," Samuel said. "You turn up here making blueprints and researching the lodge, and then Connor appears with this ridiculous injunction. Do you think I'm stupid?"

"Samuel, our firm sent us here to see about buying the lodge," Rory said, his face hardening. "We don't have any interest in tearing it down. That doesn't make any sense. We're definitely not affiliated with Caldwell."

"Did you honestly think I wouldn't figure it out?" Samuel asked, desperation growing. It seemed impossible to him that Rory would reappear in his life and put him through the emotional wringer, only for Connor Caldwell to appear and order the closure of his lodge. "Did he dig you up because he knew the effect you'd have on me?"

"What effect?" Rory asked, a glint in his eyes even as he stared at Samuel with clear irritation.

"You know," Samuel said, staring back at him. "You know. Don't pretend you don't know."

Before Rory could say anything else, Ty piped up. "Samuel, what exactly did Connor say?"

"That he had approached me a few years ago under a holding company to buy the lodge in order to tear it down and build timeshares," Samuel said. "I refused, and this is his next step, I suppose. Force me to shut the lodge down so he can buy it for pennies and ruin my livelihood." His gaze snapped back to Rory. "You really want to claim that this is a coincidence?"

"It's not a claim," Rory said. "My firm wants to buy the lodge and keep you as manager. I told you, that's why I'm here to begin with! I don't understand why you're blaming this on me." He reached out again to take the documentation, and this time Samuel let him pick it up, although he was still unconvinced. "Can I make a copy of this?"

"Why?" Samuel asked, unable to tamp down the anger burning in his chest.

"To help," Rory said, frowning at him. "Or are you fine with just waiting to be shut down?" Samuel was quiet for a moment, and Rory leaned in, his eyes narrowing. "Why don't you believe me?"

"Because I don't know you anymore," Samuel said finally. "Twenty years ago, I wouldn't have suspected you one bit, but now…. Now I don't know you at all. I don't know what kind of man you love. I don't know what kind of person you are. I don't know if you're capable of working with someone to get what you want even if it fucks me up in the process, and that not knowing is impossible for me to look past. You're not that impulsive, emotional kid I knew. You're calculating in a way I can't get over, and I wouldn't be surprised to find out that you're lying to me even now."

Rory stared at him, and Samuel wondered why he had said all of that when he could see Rory, *his* Rory right there. Sure, he'd been rankled by the kiss earlier that day, but it seemed obvious now that Rory hadn't been gloating. If Samuel considered what he'd seen in deeper detail, it was easy to tell that Rory had been looking at him to see if he was upset. He *was* impulsive—hadn't he shown it in his reactions to Samuel when he'd thought he'd been married? Just because they were older, just because they were different, didn't mean that Samuel didn't know him anymore.

But it was too late for Samuel to take back what he'd said, Rory's blank stare turning into the face of a man who was very clearly trying not to cry. "Okay," he said, voice thick, but he still held on to the document Connor had left on the desk. "I'll take a look at this and get the original back to you. Sorry," he finished, and before Samuel could say anything further, Rory had fled.

Ty cleared his throat, and Samuel realized that there had been a witness to his humiliation, his gaze snapping to the other man. "I'll, uh, talk to him," Ty offered, although Samuel couldn't imagine that Ty actually wanted to be involved in any of this. "Don't give up hope. There's no way in hell that Caldwell can get away with this."

He turned and followed Rory out of the lobby, and Samuel was left alone, a sense of dread hanging over him that was only partially to do with Connor's injunction.

Chapter Fourteen

"WHAT DO you think you can even accomplish here?"

Malcolm was sitting on the edge of his bed, pulling on a pair of thick woolen socks, with Ty perched next to him. Both of them were watching Rory, who was removing the spiral from the document while he stood near the desk in the room. He glanced at Malcolm, still steadfastly pretending that he hadn't burst into the room crying five minutes prior and interrupted Malcolm getting out of the shower. "What do you mean?"

"If the injunction is legitimate, which it seems to be, there's not much we can do to stop it. As much as it sucks, our role here is really just to collect information to present to the company. If the lodge is no longer for sale, then that's all we can report back to them."

Rory turned to look at him fully. "I'm not thinking about the company right now or our presentation. Samuel's my friend. He…. He *was* my friend. And even if I fucked that up, I can't just stand by and let him lose his business."

Malcolm considered this, and Rory could see the wheels in his head turning. Once again he was struck by the sensation that he and Malcolm had become friends. It wasn't obvious, but a trust had grown between them that hadn't been there when they'd arrived a week ago. Even the kiss earlier in the day hadn't derailed it, although the conversation with Ty had gone a long way to undoing Rory's ill feelings about that whole thing. "Fine," Malcolm said, finishing with his socks and reaching past Ty to grab a pair of winter boots. "I'll help you, but you need to be prepared to accept that the solution might be at odds with your actual job."

Rory looked down at the paperwork in his hands and frowned, steeling himself. "I have to help him. I know that I can."

"All right," Malcolm said, grabbing the keys to the rental car off the nightstand that sat between their beds and tossing them to Rory, who caught them haphazardly. "Go make a copy of the document. Ty and I have a dinner date."

"What?" Rory looked between the two of them before jabbing his finger at Ty. "What's all this about not kissing him?"

"I'm not going to kiss him," Ty said, grinning. "Jeez, you really jumped the gun there, huh? We're just having dinner together to discuss our mutual respect and admiration for one another."

Malcolm got to his feet, straightening his sweater and looking at Rory intently. "I'll help you later tonight. We need a full copy of what Connor provided, and if you have the time, you need to swing by the historical society and ask them to gather any records on the lodge. I did some preliminary research into the historical status of the building before we came, but since I didn't think it would benefit us, I let it be. I have a really strong feeling that their help is going to be instrumental in helping Samuel in turn."

Rory nodded, pocketing the keys and looking around for one of his various notebooks, but he stopped his search when Ty spoke, lingering in the doorway. "I don't think Samuel meant what he said," he offered, and Rory looked at him. "All that stuff about not knowing you. I know I don't know either of you that well, but I think he was just scared."

"Thanks, Ty," Rory said, genuinely touched. Malcolm put his hand on Ty's waist, leading him out of the room, and as soon as they were gone, Rory sank onto his own bed, clutching the car keys and the document in his hand. Now that his shock had worn off from Samuel's outburst, he was overcome by a combination of irritation and just plain sadness. The worst feeling of all was that Samuel's words had been true.

They didn't know each other anymore, and the very first thing out of Rory's mouth when he'd seen Samuel had been a lie. Since then, he'd just continued to deceive the other man, and it was clear that even if Samuel didn't know the nature of the lie, he still knew that Rory wasn't being honest. He still could feel that wall between them, and that was Rory's own fault. He had to figure out a way to fix this, had to figure out how to undo the damage he'd caused, and if he could save the lodge while doing that… well, he needed to try.

"No good lying around here moping," Rory said, grabbing his phone and checking what time the print shop closed before heading out of the room and down to the lobby. He found that Samuel was no longer on the front desk, relief flooding him before guilt followed behind, and he headed out to the parking garage. It was a clear night despite all the snow on the ground, and Rory made it to the center of town fairly quickly, found a parking spot close to the print shop, and collected his things before stepping outside onto the sidewalk.

No sooner had he done so than he heard his name. Turning, he found himself looking at Jasper and Louis, the pair of teens hand in hand and sporting matching scarves that Rory was willing to bet they hadn't had before. Suddenly aware that he was holding a document that would undoubtedly drive a rift between the pair, Rory flipped the paperwork around to hide the title page and offered them a smile. "What are you guys up to? You on a date?"

Jasper grinned, his face flushed pink, although Rory wasn't sure if it was due to the cold or pleasure from being out with Louis. "I guess so," he said as Louis nodded in agreement next to him. "We're just coming from dinner. Why are you in town this late?"

"A last-minute bit of work came in, so I'm going to the print shop," Rory said, surprised at how easily the lie came. Admitting to these teenagers that they were heading into a Romeo and Juliet situation was way more than he could stand. Besides, it was up to Samuel to break the news to Jasper; that wasn't Rory's place. "Actually, I'm glad I ran into you. Do you have a second?"

"Yeah, sure," Jasper said, glancing at Louis before turning his attention back to Rory. "Is everything okay?"

"I just wanted to ask you, um, if your father has said anything to you about how different I am than when we were kids." Rory wondered if that sounded pathetic, if fishing for information from his former boyfriend's teenage son *was* pathetic, but if it was, Jasper didn't show it on his face. Instead, he looked thoughtful, tilting his head back to think. "It's okay if you can't think of anything. I don't want to pressure you."

"You're not pressuring me," Jasper said. "He hasn't really talked to me about that much. Or, well, he has, but mostly just about how much he missed you, I guess." He paused for a moment, stepping over on the sidewalk so they weren't impeding traffic. Now underneath an awning decorated with candy-cane-striped lights, Rory had the distinct feeling that by asking the question in the first place he had opened himself up to interrogation. "Rory, come on. What's actually going on?"

"What do you mean?" Rory asked, feigning innocence. "I'm just asking a question."

"I don't think you're in love with Malcolm," Jasper said.

"Me neither," Louis said, and Rory briefly wondered how a likable kid had come from such a snake of a father. "Like, no offense, but the way he and Ty look at each other is way more believable. It's *so* romantic."

"Okay, I get it," Rory said, his frustration at the way he and Samuel had parted ways leaving him with little patience to deflect suspicion. "You can't tell your dad."

"Tell him what?" Jasper asked, taking his turn to pretend he didn't know what Rory meant.

"That Malcolm and I aren't together," Rory admitted. How many more people would figure it out before he had the chance to tell Samuel himself? "Is it really that obvious?"

"I mean, my dad hasn't figured it out, but when Malcolm kissed you earlier, you looked genuinely fucking disgusted," Jasper said. "It was not the face of a man in love. So then I started thinking about it. You really just seem to tolerate him, but my dad? He makes you feel things. Maybe not always good things, but it's more than Malcolm."

"Plus, he's just not that good at acting like he's in love with you," Louis added. "And you guys are never together. He's always with Ty, and you've been spending more time with Mr. Daniels than you have with your idiot fiancé. Not exactly a romantic holiday for you two."

Rory rubbed at his jaw, narrowing his eyes as he considered what exactly he was supposed to do. "Your dad hasn't figured it out yet?"

"No," Jasper said, shaking his head vehemently. "No, he's got no idea. I think at most he thinks Malcolm is cheating on you? But he definitely doesn't think that you're, uh, pretending to be engaged. Because honestly, that's kind of something a crazy person does."

"God, I know," Rory said. "I didn't mean to, okay? I just didn't... I didn't want your dad to think I'd just been waiting around for him for years."

"Why?" Jasper asked. "He's been doing that for you."

It was as though a lightning bolt had struck Rory, a spasm of sudden understanding. "What about your mom?"

Jasper peered at him, briefly confused, before shaking his head. "You need to ask my dad about that," he said pointedly. "In fact, you guys really need to have a serious conversation. Like, no offense, but you should have maybe had a coffee with him before you came up with the most ridiculous lie anyone has ever come up with."

"I *know*," Rory said, groaning. "Look, I'm not proud that I lied. I can't believe everyone figured it out so quickly, though."

"Do you guys even like each other, like... as friends?" Louis asked, rocking back on his heels. "Because that might not help your lack of acting skills."

"We weren't friends when we got here," Rory said. "But I think he's kind of growing on me." He looked between the teenagers, sighing softly. "Don't tell your dad, okay? I'll… I need to figure out how to tell him."

"Why? Just be honest."

"Uh…. Before I left this afternoon, he called me a liar," Rory said. "So that's complicated things. Because if I tell him now…."

"He'll only think you're more of a liar," Jasper finished, nodding slowly. "Okay, yeah, that's not great. Do you know how to fix it yet?"

"I've got an idea," Rory said. "But it'll take a little bit of doing. Can you guys just not tell Samuel until I can figure things out?"

"Oh, we're definitely not telling my dad that you're lying to him," Jasper said, putting his hands up. "You're on your own there."

"Got it," Rory said. "You guys go on. I didn't mean to interrupt your date."

"I think it was a worthwhile interruption," Louis said, laughing, and he hooked his hand back in Jasper's, the two of them heading off down the street after saying their goodbyes. Rory, who had temporarily forgotten why he had come down to town in the first place, looked at the document in his hands and sighed. Things had gone so badly so quickly.

He made his way down the sidewalk to the print shop, went inside, and explained to the woman behind the counter that he needed a copy made. She looked at the document in his hands and frowned, clearly not impressed by the sight of it, and glanced up at the clock. "It'll take about half an hour," she said, taking the papers from him and turning around to set them next to the copier. "Do you usually do your copying this late at night?"

"It was an emergency," Rory said, thoroughly chastised. "Do you have a tip jar?"

She gave him a baleful look that clearly said no, and Rory decided it was smarter for him to find a spot where he could kill half an hour rather than sit here and stare at the woman as she worked. He left the print shop and crossed the street to the still bustling cafe, ordered a hot chocolate with extra whipped cream and candy cane pieces. To be honest, it was nice to have some time to himself, to truly digest what had taken place and muddle through what he needed to do. He took the hot chocolate to go and made his way back out to the chilly street, intent on seeing more of what had changed in town since he had left all those years ago.

Downtown was mostly unchanged, the niche little shops that made Evergreen Hill such a lasting Christmas destination updated from Rory's youth but still the same at their core. Rory was peering at a model train set in the window of the toy store, a childhood spent roaming the aisles with Samuel with the impossible task of deciding how to spend their allowances. Nearly every time the result was the same: the two of them would pool their money to buy a more expensive toy, and Samuel would inevitably allow Rory to take the toy home first.

How long had Samuel been putting Rory first? How had he not recognized that someone who treated him with such clear love was incapable of breaking his heart unless forced to do so?

Rory sighed, taking another sip of his cocoa before turning away from the shop to continue his walk. Before he could, though, a certificate hanging next to the door on the inside of the glass caught his eye. He'd seen the same certificate in several other places and had chalked it up to a health inspector's report, but on a toy store that simply didn't make sense. Rory leaned in to read the certificate and immediately, like a lightning bolt from heaven, knew how he could save the lodge.

Chapter Fifteen

"WE SHOULD go," Jasper murmured, but he made no attempt to move Louis off his lap, nor did he stop himself from nipping at the other boy's throat to reinforce the hickey he had already left on the pale skin there. "We told Rory we were leaving town. If he beats us back there, my dad will have a fit."

"Stop kissing me, then," Louis said, but he also made no attempt to disentangle himself from Jasper. "And that's assuming Rory even talks to your dad. He didn't seem all that happy when we ran into him."

They were parked about halfway between town and the lodge on a dirt road that had once led to the silver mine but had long been abandoned, turning it into a popular make-out spot for Evergreen Hill's teenagers. Jasper had pushed the driver's seat back as far as it could go and had spent what felt like an eternity kissing Louis, his crush rapidly speeding toward a full-blown like. That they had only a week or so left had not yet dampened his spirits. To Jasper it seemed like ample time to figure out exactly what he wanted. Tonight, it was to make out with Louis until his lips were numb.

He had just pulled Louis down into another kiss when Louis's phone began to vibrate on the center console. He pulled back, leaning over to peer at it before making a face. "Hold on, it's my dad," he said, fishing his phone out of the cupholder and resting back on Jasper's legs. He answered the call, absently toying with the hem of Jasper's sweater. "Hey, Dad. Oh no, we're on our way back. We just stopped for dessert." He paused, looking down at Jasper. "It was really nice. I had a lot of fun."

A thrill went through Jasper, and he could feel himself turn red, his hand resting flat against Louis's thigh as he looked up at him. "Yeah, we'll be back soon. Okay, love you." With that, Louis hung up, tossed his phone onto the passenger seat, and took hold of Jasper's face. He kissed him again, soft and lingering, before seeming to muster the will to lift himself off Jasper's lap and clamber unsteadily into the passenger seat alongside his phone. "You're okay with heading back, right?"

"It's probably the responsible thing to do," Jasper said, letting out a dramatic sigh that provoked a laugh from Louis. He started the truck and pulled his seat belt across his chest, looking over at Louis, only to be surprised as Louis reached over and took hold of his hand, lacing their fingers together comfortably. "Were you telling your dad the truth?"

"About what?" Louis said, looking out the car window at the passing trees as Jasper drove them onto the main road. "About our date being nice? Yeah, of course. Dinner was delicious, the town was so cute, and I guess I enjoyed the guy I was with?"

Jasper laughed, squeezing Louis's hand gently. "He enjoyed you, I think," he said quietly. "And I don't think he's ever been on a date before that wasn't chaperoned."

"Probably good we weren't chaperoned tonight," Louis said, and Jasper could see him smiling in the window's reflection. "I don't think it would have stopped me from kissing you, though."

"Good," Jasper said, absently pressing Louis's knuckles to his lips in a soft kiss. "I think I'm starting to really like you, you know."

Louis laughed, looking over at him briefly, and in the dim light of the car's interior, Jasper thought he looked genuinely gorgeous. Unbidden, he wondered if his father had ever felt the same way looking at Rory as Jasper felt now. A weird sorrow struck him, the idea of his dad having known someone for his entire life and loving him just as long, only to lose him out of the blue. He didn't remember his mother, but he couldn't believe she would have wanted that for him.

The drive from the make-out road to the lodge was only about ten minutes, filled mostly with silence that was so comfortable Jasper sank into it with pleasure, some nondescript Christmas station playing on the radio and Louis drawing lazy patterns on the back of Jasper's hand with his thumb. As soon as they'd entered the lodge, however, that fuzzy pre-holiday feeling had fallen by the wayside, replaced by a sensation Jasper had never felt in the building before.

"What's going on?" he asked, brow furrowing as he approached the desk. His father was standing there, leafing through a mountain of paperwork, and to either side of him were Juliet and Clark, each with their own stack of papers.

Samuel looked startled, head lifting at the sound of his son's voice, and Jasper saw he was wearing his reading glasses. "Hey," he said, plastering a smile across his face. It was too late, though, Jasper having already read the stress on his father's face as though it was written in neon lights. "How was dinner?"

"Good," Jasper said, setting the truck keys on the desk. "What's going on? What's all this paper?"

"Oh, it's all the information I got when I purchased the lodge," Samuel said. His eyes flitted briefly to Louis, his smile faltering. "I'm not sure I should say anything yet."

"Oh, uh, I'll go to the restaurant," Louis said. He squeezed Jasper's hand before letting go and heading across the lobby, leaving Jasper watching his father with confusion.

"Did something happen while I was gone?" Jasper asked, a decidedly unsteady sensation overcoming him now that Louis was gone and his dad was looking at him like someone had died. As Samuel began to explain what had transpired, the unreal feeling only spread. Things began to slot into place—Rory's appearance in town and the large document under his arm—but one thing stood out to Jasper above all.

Sitting in his old treehouse in the flush of his first kiss with Louis, and Louis saying he hoped his dad kept everything the same. Jasper hadn't really paid attention to it at the time, but now it seemed clear what he had meant. Louis had known this entire time that his father was planning on springing this trap. Had he agreed to the date that night solely to keep him of the way? Had his father called not to check in on him but to let him know that the dirty deed was over?

"Jasper," Samuel said, looking at his son with concern. Jasper looked back at him, refocusing, and Samuel reached out to touch his shoulder. "It's okay," he said quietly. "I'll get this figured out. I promise."

"I know, Dad," Jasper said, forcing a smile. "Rory's helping you, then?"

Samuel's forced smile dipped briefly, a sorrow glinting in his eyes. "I doubt it," he said. "Don't worry about that right now. And don't… I don't think Louis should bear any of the blame for this. Just don't let it affect your date."

"Okay," Jasper lied, nodding carefully. "I won't. Are you gonna be okay?"

"I'll be fine. Jules and Clark are helping me out. Go finish up with Louis, yeah? You deserve to have a good night."

"Thanks," Jasper said, turning and heading across the lobby toward the restaurant. Truthfully, he didn't think he could feel sicker. His stomach was churning, anxiety prickling at the nape of his neck the closer he got to where Louis waited. Louis had known this entire time that his father was planning to pull the lodge out from underneath them, and it left Jasper questioning whether Louis even liked him at all. He didn't think he'd been mistaken about that, at least, but then again, he had no way of knowing.

Louis was sitting at the bar, chatting with the bartender and drinking what looked like a Shirley Temple. Jasper's first instinct was how cute that drink was, only to immediately have that thought swallowed up by betrayal. He approached Louis slowly, trying to put off the inevitable but unable to do so for long. Louis grinned at him when he saw him, although that expression rapidly faltered when he saw Jasper's face. "What happened?'

"Did you know?" Jasper asked, unable to keep his voice from shaking slightly.

"Know what?" Louis said, peering at him. "What's going on?"

"When I took you up to my treehouse, you said something about hoping your dad kept the lodge the same," Jasper said, his hand resting on the bar top as he looked down at Louis. By this point, the bartender had moved away, and Jasper was glad there were no prying eyes or ears, embarrassed by how heightened his emotions were. "My dad just told me that while we were gone, your dad served him with a notice to close the lodge because it's jutting onto the boundary of the silver mine."

Louis went pale, his brow furrowing as he tried to figure out what he was being told. "A notice to close the lodge?" he repeated, visibly confused. "I don't…. That's not what he told me."

"Then what did he tell you?" Jasper asked, seething. The logical part of his brain was sure Louis wasn't a good enough actor to play dumb like this, and yet he wasn't relying on logic right now.

"That he wanted to buy the lodge and thought your dad would agree because you were getting to be college-aged," Louis said, his drink abandoned as he turned to face Jasper fully. "He told me he wanted to keep your dad on as manager because he's obviously good at it. Are you sure your dad is interpreting things correctly?"

"Yes," Jasper said, voice strained. "I'm positive. He's going through every last bit of paperwork he's ever gotten to see if he has a leg to stand on." He paused for the briefest of moments, unable to stop the words that came from him next. "Did you just go out with me tonight to make sure I wasn't around when your dad dropped the bombshell? Did you even want to go on a date?"

"Excuse me?" Louis stared at him, visibly stunned, and despite knowing full well that it was too late to take back what he said, Jasper realized immediately that he had gone too far. "Are you seriously asking me if I went on a date with you because I wanted to or because my dad coerced me?"

He got to his feet, still staring at Jasper, who managed to say, "I didn't mean it like that," before Louis took a handful of his shirt, shooting him a decidedly dirty look. Turning, Louis kept a hold on Jasper as he led him through the restaurant to the huge French door that led out to the heated patio, bustling with skiers fresh off the slopes. Louis kept going, stepping off onto the cobblestone path that branched toward the resort and back around toward the front of the lodge.

Once they were about halfway around the building Louis stopped in a natural nook, pushing Jasper so his back was up against the external wall. "I didn't think we should fight in the restaurant," he said, but there was a cold quality to his voice that hadn't been there before. "Were you being serious back there?"

"About what part?" Jasper asked, but some of his bravado had been replaced by uncertainty. If Louis didn't like him, if he'd been put up to all of this by his dad, then certainly he wouldn't look this upset.

"What part?" Louis repeated, his voice slightly shriller than he normally sounded. "You're joking. You have to be. Do you honestly think my dad told me to make out in a truck with you for half an hour? In an Armani sweater?"

Jasper stared at him, his mouth going dry. His dad had point-blank told him that Louis hadn't been involved, and Jasper had ignored him, and now he was looking his crush in the face and realizing he had totally misjudged things. Everything he liked about Louis—his sense of humor, his forthright nature, his easy intelligence—made it damn near impossible to believe he would go on a date with Jasper at his father's bidding. His temper had gotten the better of him, and of course he was only realizing it now, far too late.

"Louis," he said, reaching out to grab one of Louis's hands, only for the other boy to pull his arm out of reach. "Man, I'm sorry. I got so mad thinking about what your dad did that I—"

"That you accused me of being some kind of… I don't even know what word to use. Seductress?" Louis was visibly hurt, hugging himself tightly around the middle and looking at Jasper. "I'm not my dad, you know. He told me he wanted to buy the place. Why wouldn't I believe him?"

"I'm sorry," Jasper said, but even he could see this conversation was a runaway train he had no hope of keeping on the rails. "I didn't think—"

"This fucking sucks," Louis said. "I had a really nice time tonight, but you don't even trust me, do you."

"That's not it," Jasper said, taking a step forward, only for Louis to take a step back in response. "Come on."

"I need some time to figure this out," he said, putting his hands up. "I really need to think this over, so just…. Just don't talk to me for a bit." Louis gave Jasper one last baleful look before turning and walking back in the direction of the restaurant.

Jasper stood there in the cold for a few long moments, staring up at the fat, fluffy snow beginning to drift down from the clouded night sky. He was an idiot, a serious fucking idiot, and it finally dawned on him as he turned and started to walk toward the front of the lodge to avoid following Louis. He had just rounded the corner to the main drive when he spotted Rory exiting the underground parking garage. He was holding a pastry box, his plaid scarf pulled up over his chin, and he spotted Jasper almost at the exact same time. "Hey," he said, slightly muffled. "Your date went well?"

Jasper couldn't stop himself. The moment Rory spoke, it was as though a floodgate had been lifted. Tears welled up in his eyes and he shook his head, registering the panic on Rory's face but unable to stop himself from crying.

Chapter Sixteen

THE PRINT shop woman had been in a much better mood when Rory had returned to pick up his order, a change that had come from his arrival with a half-dozen tarts from the cafe. After all, she had been the reason he'd hit upon his epiphany in the first place. With his copy and another dozen tarts for those he cared about at the lodge in tow, Rory had driven back up the mountain, considering the whole time whether the idea he'd had was the same one Malcolm had alluded to.

It must have been, a solution both guaranteed to work and that would put Rory at odds with the architectural firm. Rory mulled this over as he approached, snow just barely beginning to fall as he reached the underground lot. Balancing the pastry box and the documents, he bundled up and made his way to the front doors. Underneath the awning he spotted Jasper, eyes widening a little in recognition. "Hey," he said, surprised to see the teenager out here by himself. He hadn't been on a date in a while, but based on his interaction with Jasper and Louis in town, he'd have thought they would have been glued to one another. "Your date went well?"

Immediately, mystifyingly, Jasper began to cry. Rory stared at him, flabbergasted, before fumbling with what he was carrying to free one of his hands. "Hey," he said again, this time in the tone of someone trying very hard to stop a kid from crying. "Hey, come on, don't cry. What's going on?" Jasper shook his head, tilting his head back like he thought it might stem the flow of tears, and Rory frowned. "Should I go get your dad?"

"No!" Jasper said, looking at Rory. "No, he specifically told me not to do something, and I did it anyway. He'll be so disappointed in me."

Based on what Rory had seen, he didn't think that, but he also kind of remembered how it was to be a teenager. "Okay, no problem," he said, putting a hand on Jasper's shoulder in an attempt to comfort him. "Come on, uh… is there a way to get inside without Samuel seeing us? Because if he sees you crying, he's going to want to talk to you."

Jasper rubbed at his face. "Yeah, follow me," he said, sniffling as he led Rory back to the restaurant path and around the far side of the lodge. They entered the door usually reserved for delivery personnel, and Jasper pushed into an office that had Juliet's name on the door but seemed rarely used. He collapsed into a chair and kicked another one out for Rory.

Rory settled into the chair, which was weirdly lumpy, and set the items he'd been carrying down on the seldom-used desk. "Okay," he said, looking at the teenager steadily. "What's going on? You seemed totally fine when I saw you in town earlier. Did something happen?"

Jasper hunched over himself, pressing the heels of his palms into his eye sockets to try and stop the tears. "Ugh," he said, voice thick with emotion. "I don't usually cry, I promise."

"You don't need to be ashamed of crying," Rory said quickly. "Cry as much as you need to, just, uh, tell me what's going on so I can decide if I actually need to tell your dad. Because if you're crying because you murdered someone, I feel like I probably should tell Samuel." As Rory had hoped, that got a snort out of Jasper, who forced himself to sit up straight. "Come on, spill."

"It's so stupid. I'm so stupid. We had a really nice night, and, like, I know that it's too soon for it to be anything more than like, but I like him. And we were, uh, parked, and his dad called, so we came back to the lodge, and then my dad told me what had happened, and I got so caught up in thinking that…. That he didn't like me for real. This stupid nagging little voice saying he's traveled all over, lived in New York, has definitely met people way more interesting than me."

Rory listened, able to connect the dots pretty easily. He opened the pastry box, removed a small chocolate tart, and held it out to Jasper, who looked confused but took it nonetheless. "Can I tell you a story?" he asked, looking at the teenager for a few long moments, seeing very clearly Samuel at the same age.

"Is it about you and my dad?"

"Yeah," Rory said, and Jasper nodded. "We would have been in tenth grade, I think. By that point, we'd been together for about two years, and your grandparents knew, but I don't think anyone else really did. Your dad and I were relatively popular, but because of Samuel's personality and size, he was constantly being asked to join teams. We did track together, but it wasn't really something we took seriously, so I think we were both surprised when he got asked to join the football team."

Jasper snorted again, wiping his thumb over the apple of his cheek to brush away the last of his tears. "Did they realize what a bad idea that was?"

"Not at first," Rory said, laughing. "Samuel figured it would be fine because he was just supposed to be replacing a guy with a temporary injury. It cut down on the time we could spend together, but I had started a new job at the bookstore that summer, so it wasn't that horrible at first. On the days I had off, I'd just do some work at the school library until he was done with practice."

Rory laughed suddenly, a slightly embarrassed sound that foreshadowed how things had gone. "There was this senior on the team that was ridiculously hot. He was nice too, and looking back I think he just realized Samuel was terrible at football, so he was trying to give him a hand. I started to get jealous almost immediately, convinced that this guy was going to steal Samuel. Like, Samuel had never shown a single inkling he was interested in anyone else, but I was so jealous, so worked up. Then one Friday I show up to meet him after practice, and this guy is holding your dad in his arms, full Renaissance painting. I don't even remember how I got home except that I must have because I spent the rest of the weekend holed up at my place, miserable."

Jasper was staring at him, the chocolate tart sitting half-finished on the desk in front of him. "My dad hasn't told me this story," he said, incredulous. "You thought he was cheating on you with some football star?"

"Yeah, until Sunday night when he realizes I'm ignoring all his phone calls and shows up on my porch with a boot on his right leg. He finally gets the truth out of me, and while I'm getting more and more upset, he just starts laughing. As it turns out, on Friday he broke his fucking ankle at practice, and I turned up in the direct aftermath. I misinterpreted things so badly that I left my boyfriend there with a broken ankle, and his dad had to come get him instead. I'm lucky Samuel thought the whole thing was funny, but I'm sure you can tell why I decided this was the story to tell you."

Jasper was quiet for a moment, picking at the crust of the tart. "You guys were already together for ages at that point, but you still felt insecure," he said finally. "Like you weren't enough. How did you fix it?"

"I made myself listen to your dad and believe what he was saying," Rory said. "If he didn't like me, he wouldn't be with me. The same is true for Louis. When I saw you two earlier, I didn't see a kid who was there because he didn't want to be. Sometimes letting someone else override that shitty voice inside your head is okay."

Jasper considered this, seeming to really mull it over, and Rory thought the boy's demeanor grew a little less doom and gloom. "I get it," he said, nodding. "Who was the football player, by the way?"

Rory felt genuinely embarrassed at this question, rubbing awkwardly at the side of his neck. "It was Clark," he admitted, and this got a full laugh from Jasper, who no longer seemed on the verge of tears. "Maybe that's why your dad never told you. I don't think Clark knows how jealous I was of him for a while there."

"That's honestly so funny," Jasper said, grinning at Rory. "I think it's because my dad talked about you so much, but you're really easy to talk to. I always wanted to meet you and see if my dad was just romanticizing things, but he really was spot-on." He paused, a solemnity crossing his face that made him look nearly identical to his father. "Why did you never come back? I think my dad always thought you would at least visit."

Rory crossed his arms over his chest, eyes fixated on a ceiling vent just above Jasper's head. "I thought I didn't have anything to come back to. I thought—and I know I'm wrong now—that your dad didn't follow me because he didn't want me in his life anymore. So I just decided it was better to cut my losses, and not look back because it was too much to bear."

"What about your family?" Jasper asked. "Actually, I don't think my dad has ever mentioned your parents, and I've never met them."

"You wouldn't have," Rory said. "My parents never really took having a kid seriously. We were well off, but my dad was an executive at some tech company, and my mom was a pilot. I was raised mostly by nannies and your grandparents, to be honest. When I was in seventh grade, my mom died in a car accident. My dad was never the same, and I got myself legally emancipated at sixteen. I think he's in England now, if he's still alive."

It was a story that had long ago lost its sting for Rory. His mother was only the faintest memory, the misery of hearing about her death numbed by the fact that he had spent the night in the rec room the Danielses had installed in their basement, that it had been the first time he and Samuel had kissed. That recollection, as bad at kissing as they had both been, softened the edges of the first big tragedy of Rory's life. When he lowered his gaze, however, Jasper looked like he was going to cry again. "What's wrong?" Rory asked, alarmed, and Jasper shook his head, stuffing some of the tart into his mouth. "Jasper?"

"It just makes me so sad to think about," Jasper said. "That you've gone twenty years without people you loved and vice versa. My grandparents have a graduation picture of you that's hanging on their wall, and all kinds of stuff my dad says you left behind. Did you give my grandma a cardigan for Christmas one year?"

Rory nodded, frowning. He had given it to Marion the last Christmas he had been in town, when he'd been accepted to NYU on early acceptance and hadn't told anyone yet, not even Samuel. The cardigan had been beautiful, hand-knit by a local woman, and he'd gotten John, her husband, a matching toque and scarf. "What about it?"

"She still has it," Jasper said. "It's been fixed a dozen times, but if anyone says she should throw it out, she says she can't because it's one of the nicest gifts she's ever gotten. I really think that you leaving left a kind of hole in our family. I've definitely felt it my whole life, even if I never knew you in the flesh. I think you'd be surprised by how loved you still are here."

Rory wanted to refute all that, wanted to argue that Samuel thought him an insincere liar so radically changed by city life that he would side with a man using legal trickery to essentially steal a building during Christmastime like some overeager Grinch. If he made that argument, though, he would be undoing the point he had just made about ignoring that shitty part of his brain telling him he wasn't good enough. "Your grandparents really are the ones who made me love Christmas," he said instead, a deflection from the real meaning of Jasper's words: that Samuel might still love him. "They always made me feel so welcome. I never really liked the holidays until I started spending them at the bed and breakfast, you know?"

Jasper looked at him, his chocolate tart finished. "Okay, can we make a promise to each other?"

"I'm not buying you beer."

Jasper grinned, shaking his head. "I'm a high school senior, you know. I don't need some dork from the city buying me beer."

"A dork!" Rory said, laughing. "Jesus. Okay, what's the promise?"

"If I ignore the voice telling me Louis can do better, you ignore the voice telling you my dad doesn't care about you anymore. Fair?"

"Fair," Rory said, pushing himself to his feet and offering his hand for Jasper to shake. The teen shook it, hopping to his feet as well and looking down at Rory. "I won't tell your dad what happened."

"I won't tell my dad that Malcolm isn't your fiancé," Jasper said, stifling a yawn. He started for the office door and then stopped, turning to look at Rory again. "I really like you," he said with disarming sincerity. "I think my childhood would have been even better with you there."

There were a dozen things Rory could have said in return—that he thought the same thing, that he felt a kinship with Jasper that surprised him—but he just smiled and said, "There's time to make up for it now."

As soon as Jasper had left the office, though, and Rory turned his attention back to the copy he had made, he couldn't help but wonder if he had promised more than he could possibly deliver.

Chapter Seventeen

THERE WAS a Do Not Disturb sign on the doorknob of his room. Rory stared at it in utter disbelief, clutching the pastry box in his arms and his hotel key in his right hand. "What the fuck?" he whispered, paralyzed by indecision and irritation. Finally he decided to knock, only because the thought of catching Malcolm and Ty knocking boots was exhausting after the day he'd had. "Malcolm, open the door," he murmured, glancing down the hallway, only to turn back when the door opened. To his horror, Malcolm was shirtless.

"Oh, hi," Malcolm said, leaning against the jamb and blocking Rory from seeing in the room. "Look, just give me an hour." Rory heard the shower turn on, and a strange gleam came into Malcolm's eyes. Rory realized that Malcolm was horny. "Maybe two."

"What happened to no kissing? This is a lot more than kissing!"

"Yeah, it is," Malcolm said, his usually tempered Scottish accent slipping into a broader brogue. He looked down at Rory, the faintest smile ghosting the corner of his lips. "Have you ever believed in love at first sight?"

Rory, whose only true love had been created over years, peered up at him. "Have you?"

"Now? Absolutely," Malcolm sighed. "Give me two hours. We couldn't go to his room because it's in the staff quarters now."

Another fallout from Rory's monstrously stupid lie. He was getting used to this feeling now. "If I don't cockblock you, then tomorrow you help me with my idea for saving the lodge," he challenged, wondering when he had gotten comfortable with Malcolm to the extent where he was willing to banter about sex while angling for assistance at the same time.

"Fine," Malcolm said.

Rory pushed the pastries and documents into Malcolm's arms, frowning. "Don't have sex on my bed," he said. "And give me the book from my suitcase."

Malcolm disappeared into the room briefly with Rory's things and returned with the cheap paperback thriller Rory had brought but hadn't started. He handed it over, glancing back at the bathroom briefly before asking something Rory genuinely didn't think Malcolm was capable of caring about. "Are you feeling better?" he asked, turning his pale eyes onto Rory. "You were really upset earlier."

"I am feeling better, yeah, thanks," Rory said, surprised. "I talked to Jasper. The kid is surprisingly down to earth, but I guess Samuel was at that age too. I was always the flighty one."

"I'm not going to tell you what to do, but if I was in your shoes, I wouldn't bother holing up with that shitty book somewhere. I'd go and talk to Samuel." The shower stopped behind him, and that hungry gleam came back into his eyes. "I'll text you when we're done."

"Disgusting," Rory said mockingly, Malcolm shoving his head back through the door as playfully as he was capable of being. With his book in hand, Rory made his way downstairs to the sitting area in the lobby. Samuel was nowhere to be seen, the girl behind the desk clearly a seasonal worker, and for about half an hour Rory was able to stick to his original plan of reading. The roaring fireplace, the pleasant Christmas music, the ability to people watch whenever the admittedly shitty book lost his attention…. It was honestly the most relaxed he'd been in a long time.

At the back of his mind, however, was Samuel. There was no harm in going to see him, was there? Rory checked his watch. It was a quarter to ten, and unless Samuel was secretly a ninety-year-old man, Rory highly doubted he was asleep yet. Even if it was just to tell him he had made the copy…. But Rory knew he wanted to look Samuel in the eyes and see if there was still betrayal there. The way he'd been that afternoon, the utter disbelief and indignation…. Rory had to know whether it was fleeting or not.

He dog-eared the book—a bad habit but one he'd never managed to shake—and got to his feet. He peered at himself in the reflection of one of the huge lodge windows, flattening down the rumpled stomach of his cream-colored knit sweater. Everything else was fine, his natural curls in place and his eyes, alert and bright, looking back at him. Thank God he had his looks going for him, because he had definitely dropped the ball in terms of personality since he'd come back to town.

He walked over to the front desk, offering the girl a smile, but before he could say a word, she was appraising him. "Are you Rory?"

Caught off guard, he gawped at her briefly before recovering his senses. "How did you know that?"

The girl did a pretty good impression of Jasper. "If a handsome Black guy comes around looking for my dad, tell him where he is. He's my future stepdad."

Rory felt himself blush, groaning slightly. "Oh my God. Why would he say that to you?"

She grinned, shrugging. "I don't know. But why did you come over here?"

"To ask where Samuel is," Rory admitted, and the girl laughed.

"He's in the kitchen," she said, gesturing to the now familiar doors behind her. "I think he's making biscuits for the morning."

Baking seemed to be Samuel's stress relief, much like poring over blueprints filled the same niche for Rory. "I appreciate it," he said, rapping his knuckles against the desk before stepping around it toward the kitchen. There was no time to truly think about what Jasper had told the desk girl, and that was probably for the best. Rory had sunk hours as a boy into imagining marrying Samuel, and getting sucked back into that fantasy would put an end to what he was aiming to do at the moment.

There was a sad '90s song playing from a tinny Bluetooth speaker as Rory entered the kitchen, and he quickly spotted the source. Samuel was standing at a long steel table, working dough with a bench scraper and clearly focusing on the work. His Christmas sweater was rolled up to the elbows, an equally Christmassy apron protecting it from the dough. He looked impossibly handsome, his curls pushed back out of his eyes by a hair band, and Rory watched him work for a few stolen moments, memorized the muscles moving in Samuel's forearms in case he didn't get a second chance.

Samuel pushed the scraper forward with such vigor that a lump of not-quite-incorporated dough rolled off the edge of the table and onto the floor. As Samuel leaned forward to follow the trajectory of the dough, he spotted Rory, freezing where he stood like a rabbit hoping he hadn't been spotted by a fox. Rory took a step forward, mouth dry. "Um, I just wanted to let you know I took a copy of the document," he said. "I'll get the original back to you tomorrow if that's okay."

"Oh, okay," Samuel said, still staring at him. Rory waited for him to say more, but Samuel genuinely looked afraid, although the hurt and betrayal that had been there earlier had disappeared.

"Okay," Rory said, a little disappointed as he turned to leave the kitchen. He didn't want to hang out and read for another hour or so, but he could also tell that Samuel didn't want him there.

He had nearly reached the door when Samuel spoke. "Rory, wait." Rory turned back to look at him, surprised but secretly pleased, and tilted his head inquisitively. Before he could ask why he'd been stopped, Samuel nodded at the dough. "Do you know how to cut out biscuits?"

"No," Rory admitted, approaching him. "If you show me, though, I think I can figure it out."

"Good enough," Samuel said, looking around. "Jasper usually helps me, but he snuck past me tonight. Can't blame him. I think he's stressed." He met Rory's eyes, fine wrinkles visible at the corners, and Rory was struck again by how truly handsome he found Samuel still. "Come around to this side and roll your sleeves up."

Rory did as he was told, rolling his sleeves up and stepping into place alongside Samuel. He looked up at him, expectant, only for Samuel to take hold of his left hand and raise it. Without saying anything, he rolled Rory's sleeve up farther, past his elbow. He did it with so much tenderness that a chill went through Rory, a flame of desire licking at his heart. Samuel let go of his left arm, and Rory raised his right without needing to be asked. Samuel clasped it in his hands, fingers splayed against the soft underside of Rory's arm for a few brief moments before he rolled that sleeve up as well. Rory wondered if Samuel could feel his pulse humming rabbit-fast under his skin. "There," Samuel said, allowing his fingertips to linger on Rory's bare elbow before finally letting go. "Go wash your hands."

Hands washed and a spare apron tied around his waist, Rory took his place alongside Samuel, looking down at the dough. "They smell really good," he said, looking up at Samuel. "Do you make them every night?"

"No, we only really have biscuits with breakfast a few times a week," Samuel said, patting the huge slab of dough lightly. "Usually Jules handles it, but I needed to blow off some steam." He met Rory's gaze and smiled, although Rory could see that he was still closed off. Truthfully, the fact that he could read Samuel so easily even after all this time apart was frightening. Part of him felt like he had never left Evergreen Hill, while the rest of him feared that the man he'd become in the interim was incompatible with who Samuel was now.

Samuel walked Rory through what he needed done, and they set up an impromptu conveyor belt, Samuel making and rolling out the dough and Rory steadfastly punching biscuits out with a circle cutter. They worked in silence for fifteen minutes or so, Rory marinating in anxiety as he loaded biscuits onto a tray and tried to pretend the miserable '90s playlist Samuel had on wasn't driving him crazy.

They both hit their limit at the same time, Rory looking up from the cookie cutter and saying, "Samuel, I—"

At the exact moment he did that, Samuel set down the bench scraper and turned to face him, a desperation in his eyes that struck Rory like an arrow to the heart. "Rory, you—"

They stared at each other, Samuel's face turning pink and Rory suddenly hyperaware he was closer to Samuel than he had been in decades. "What were you going to say?" Samuel asked, braver than Rory could be.

"I'm sorry," Rory said, unable to close the floodgate now that it had opened. "I'm sorry for showing up here and thinking that I could avoid you, and I'm sorry if I did something to make you think I would work against the lodge, against you, because I wouldn't. Even being here for my firm makes me uncomfortable, but I wouldn't ever stoop to such dirty tactics and—"

Samuel, in an echo of something he'd done a million times when he and Rory had been growing up, put his hand over Rory's mouth to stop him from talking. He smelled like flour and the cheddar cheese he'd grated into the dough, and while it certainly wasn't a romantic smell, it filled Rory with an impossible desire. "Sorry," Samuel said, pulling his hand back and grabbing a clean tea towel from a nearby rack. "I got flour all over your face. I just…. You don't need to apologize, Rory. I shouldn't have said that to you, not in a million years. I got freaked out by the idea of the lodge being lost to me, and I overreacted and took it out on you."

Rory looked up at him, a surge of affection catching him entirely off guard. "I still need to say sorry," he said plainly. "I've always thought that if we ever met again, the circumstances would be different. But since I've been back, it feels like nothing I've said or done is the right thing at all. Like…. Like even just coming here by accident has caused you harm."

Samuel looked down at him, contemplative, a frown tugging at his lips. "What caused me harm was not having you here, Rory. Twenty years without you. Did you miss me at all?"

"Every fucking day," Rory said vehemently, the passion that sparked in his voice unmistakable. "I thought about you every day. It's been impossible not to. I could go another twenty years without you, and you would still consume my thoughts, Samuel. I can't—"

But what Rory couldn't do, Samuel wouldn't ever hear. He had been looking at Rory with a growing intensity, gripping the edge of the workbench with a white-knuckled fist, and he was finally unable to stop himself. He reached out, grabbing Rory by the front of his sweater and hauling him forward. He kissed Rory so hard their teeth knocked together, and if anyone else had kissed him like that, Rory would have immediately pushed them off. Samuel, though.... Samuel kissing him like that brought back a flood of memories—a clumsy first kiss the night his mother had died, a kiss at prom, a hundred shared memories that had been put on hold but now seemed as though they could resume.

Instinctively, Rory raised his hands to hold on to Samuel's apron, closing his eyes and leaning into the kiss. He parted his lips, kissed back, lost himself entirely in the sensation of Samuel's mouth on his own.... And then became aware of something vibrating in his pocket. Reality crashed down like a curtain, and Rory pulled back, staring up at Samuel and trying to ignore how full and pink Samuel's lips were now.

His phone vibrated again, and Rory touched his pocket, knowing full well it was Malcolm telling him that he could come back to the room. "Malcolm," he said by way of explanation, searching Samuel's face. "I should go."

Once again, Rory ran, a peculiar sickness swelling up inside him.

Chapter Eighteen

SAMUEL COULDN'T remember the last time he had been in such a terrible mood this close to Christmas.

He rolled onto his side, staring out the bay window in his bedroom at the snow that had been falling lazily all night. When he had purchased the lodge, it had come with a staff quarters, including the suite where he and Jasper now lived. Over the years, Samuel had renovated the space so it felt as close to a real house as he could make it. Part of that had involved installing the window in his room, but if he was honest with himself, honest the way he truly needed to be, he had added the window not for himself but for Rory.

He was such an idiot. There was a ghost of Rory in everything he had done. They had both loved the lodge as teenagers, so he had bought it. Rory had spent hours curled up in front of the bay window at the Danielses' bed and breakfast, doing homework and admiring the scenery. Rory's return had led to a revelation on Samuel's end, one that seemed far too late. For nearly twenty years he had been waiting. Waiting when he could have sought Rory out, when he could have changed things, but now he was out of time with both Rory and the lodge.

Samuel twisted the wedding ring he wore, another symbol of Rory's ghost. He wore it to fend off being hit on, but perhaps part of him still thought he was taken. The handful of dates he'd been on as an adult had left him entirely tepid, paling in comparison to his first love. And the kiss…. Samuel groaned, pressing his hands to his face as he recalled his moment of abject stupidity the night before. He'd kissed Rory like an idiot, disregarding the fact that he had a fiancé, and he really didn't think there was any coming back from that.

The door to his room opened, the creak of the hinges recognizable before a weight pressed down on the far side of his bed. "Dad?"

Samuel rolled over, looking up at Jasper. His son was dressed in the pseudo-uniform of the lodge, a flannel and jeans, and he looked as tired as Samuel felt. "Hey, kiddo," he murmured, reaching up and pushing Jasper's curls out of his face. "I know why I look like shit. Why do you?"

"I messed up last night," Jasper said.

"That seems to be going around," Samuel said, pushing himself into a sitting position. At Jasper's inquisitive look, he waved his hand. "Don't worry about it. What happened with you?"

Jasper flopped down face-first on the bed, groaning loudly. "I messed up with Louis," he said, muffled against the comforter. "And the worst part is I made a promise to Rory that I would fix it, but I don't know if I can."

"You made a promise to Rory?" Samuel echoed, an image springing unbidden to his mind of Jasper as a baby, Rory there the way Samuel had so badly wanted him to be. "When did you do that?"

"After I got back from the date last night," Jasper said. "Did he not talk to you last night?"

Samuel stared at his son, guilt creeping over him like ivy. "He came to apologize to me," he said slowly. "He promised to talk to me if you talked to Louis, is that right?"

"Uh, sort of," Jasper said. "Did he really not come to see you?"

"No, he did," Samuel admitted, his face flushing. "And I might have kissed him before he could say anything important."

Jasper was dead quiet for a moment before turning his head, staring up at his dad. "You kissed him?" he asked, stunned. "Like, actually kissed him?"

"Like actually kissed him," Samuel said, squeezing his eyes closed. "I didn't mean to. He was talking to me and it was like I'd been possessed and I just kissed him."

"Did he, uh.... Did he kiss you back?"

Samuel furrowed his brow, concentrating on what had happened before nodding. "Yeah, he did. But then Malcolm texted him, and I think he realized what he'd done." He opened his eyes, knowing he should feel guilty for having kissed Rory but only wanting to do it all over again. "Your father is a homewrecker."

Jasper was looking at him curiously, hazel eyes narrowed, and Samuel thought he was about to be told off when Jasper sat up straight. "I think you should invite him to dinner."

Samuel stared at him, uncomprehending, before the meaning sunk in. "Dinner tonight? Christmas dinner?"

"Well, Christmas Eve Eve dinner, yeah," Jasper said. "I think Grandma and Grandpa would be pretty happy to see him."

Samuel considered that, chewing at the inside of his lip. Since buying the lodge, he and Jasper celebrated Christmas dinner with his parents two days early in order to spend Christmas itself with guests. "They would be thrilled, yeah, but…."

"But what?" Jasper asked. "You kissed him. You can't tell me you don't still have feelings for him, Dad."

"I don't want Malcolm to come, that's all," Samuel said.

"Oh yeah," Jasper said, but he had that weird look in his eyes again. "Don't worry about that, I think. He's doing some project with that photographer, and Rory said he's helping with the injunction now too. He won't want to come to dinner."

"Are you going to ask Louis?"

"I don't know about that," Jasper said. "I'll, uh, think about it and let Grandma know. Anyway, I switched shifts with one of the girls so she could go skiing, so I have to go. I just wanted to make sure you hadn't died or something."

"Not dead, just heartsick," Samuel said, flopping over backward. "I'll be out in a bit."

"Okay, depressing," Jasper said, leaning over to press a kiss to his dad's forehead before disappearing.

It took all of Samuel's willpower to drag himself out of bed, the feeling of grime from being in the kitchen the night prior finally more than he could stand. He showered and dressed, mulling over Jasper's idea as he did. His parents would be thrilled to see Rory. When he'd told them Rory was back in town his mother had cried, but they had both agreed to wait and see if Rory reached out to them. Now, though, Samuel couldn't help but wonder if that had been a mistake.

Maybe waiting, maybe standing back and not chasing Rory had led to all of this. Had Malcolm chased him? Had Rory fallen for him, not because he'd given Rory space but because he'd given him none? Samuel had not followed him to New York, had not chased him down when he could have. Even now he was passive, the one bold thing he'd done kissing Rory, only to immediately be rebuffed.

He made himself a coffee, a realization overcoming him bit by bit. He couldn't accept this. He couldn't accept it until he heard it from Rory, heard that Rory no longer loved him one iota. He stared down at the coffee, at his ring, heart aching the way it only seemed to when Rory was involved. He had felt it the night prior, had been certain as anything that Rory had wanted to be kissed. Samuel still knew him, even if it ate him up inside to think they had missed so much of each other's lives, and he knew Rory had liked it. "Fuck," he whispered softly, his coalescing desires leaving him with no way to go but forward. He had to say something, simply because keeping quiet had only left him with regrets in the past. He pulled on a cardigan and headed out of their quarters, stopping briefly in the kitchen to check how Juliet was doing before beginning his daily tasks.

Running a lodge suited him, the methodical nature of the daily routine something he could do with his eyes closed. Sure, there were the occasional disgruntled guests to deal with, the rare emergency or two that cropped up from time to time, but for the most part things stayed the same. Normally his work made him happy, but this morning was different, a fog settling over Samuel's head. He sequestered himself in his office, fixating on the uncertainty of the situation with the Caldwells and the feelings he had for Rory that he simply couldn't shake now that they'd been reignited.

He'd been in there for about half an hour, working on the plans for the visit with Santa he had set up for the next afternoon, when a rapid-fire knock came at the office door. Samuel blinked, used to his employees just letting themselves in. "Um, it's open," he said, hoping against hope it wasn't Connor Caldwell there to pile more bad news on his shoulders.

Instead, Malcolm pushed his way into the office. Impeccably dressed in an Armani sweater, he looked runway ready, a revelation that made jealousy lurch violently in Samuel's chest. Malcolm was holding a stack of papers, including the document Rory had copied the night prior, and Samuel wondered if Rory had sent him down because he didn't want to face Samuel himself.

They stared at each other for a moment before Malcolm pointed at the chair opposite Samuel at the desk. "Can I sit?"

"Oh, yeah," Samuel said, straightening up where he sat. "Sorry, I was kind of expecting more bad news."

"This might be," Malcolm said, and for a heart-stopping moment Samuel was sure Rory had told Malcolm they'd kissed. Instead of alluding to that, however, Malcolm dropped into the empty chair and spread the documents out. "I have to tell you this because it will ultimately be your decision, but you need to know all the facts. Rory is going to give you the same pitch, but he's going to lie to you."

"Lie to me about what?" Samuel asked, peering down at the documents. "How are you so sure about that?"

"Because his critical thinking goes straight out the window where you're involved," Malcolm said matter-of-factly, a change clearly having come over him since the night prior. His eyes, which had been intense before, now seemed lit by a deeper fire, a grit and drive in his actions that had not been there during Samuel's brief interactions with him until now. "We have a solution for your lodge, but if you decide to go through with it, Rory will lose his job. He's going to come down here and sell you on it, but he'll leave out that part of it."

"Why would he lose his job?" Samuel asked, alarmed.

"We came here to assess your lodge and make you an offer to buy it if we liked what we saw." Malcolm pushed a pamphlet toward him, and Samuel recognized it as one of the ones he kept by the front desk for guests to decide on local attractions. "Rory's idea is to petition the historical society to have the lodge declared a protected historical building. This would codify the land agreement you've been operating under and prevent Caldwell from having the legal ground to stand on. However—"

"It would remove the option for future renovations," Samuel said, the historical society's pamphlet open in front of him. "So your company would be unable to update the lodge the way they intended."

"Exactly," Malcolm said. "This lodge and the ski resort are an extremely high-priority item for our firm, and if Rory purposefully sinks the deal, it will ruin his career. He'll either lose all credibility or his job."

"Why would he propose this as a solution if it's going to cost him so much?"

Malcolm stared at him, a blank look on his face before it was replaced by irritation. "Really? Are you actually that stupid?"

"Whoa, hey," Samuel said, putting his hands up. "That's uncalled for."

"No, I think it's perfectly called for," Malcolm said, getting to his feet. "Look, I've given you all the information I have. Figure out what you want to do with it, Samuel. If this isn't resolved by Christmas Day, I'm going to burn this place down myself."

With that threat he left the office, Samuel running his hand over the documents he'd been given. He was grateful Malcolm had come to him, but he was also confused as to why he'd done so. Why the hell would Rory risk his career like this? And why did Malcolm feel the need to intervene? He hadn't pushed Samuel one way or the other, and in fact Samuel got the sense that Malcolm was resigned to what might happen. But the possibility of Rory losing his job filled Samuel, not with trepidation, but with a weird sort of hope. If Rory was willing to risk his career for the lodge, then the reason why might be obvious. Maybe that, combined with Jasper's insistence that they invite Rory to dinner, was pointing to something it seemed almost impossible to hope for.

Samuel read over what Malcolm had brought him, seeing a clear path forward for the lodge. Having it declared a historical landmark would save them, but getting it done before the injunction came into play was going to be difficult. They were running out of time, Rory having scrawled the holiday hours for the historical society on the back of the pamphlet in the same messy handwriting he had once used for love notes passed between classes. They had today, tomorrow until 4:00 p.m., and then no chance until the twenty-seventh. That seemed like cutting it close.

Samuel sighed, resting his forehead against his knuckles and peering down at the papers. He frowned, trying to make sense of the dozen different things on his plate, only for a knock to come at the door. "Oh, come in," Samuel said, looking up, and he was both surprised and entirely not surprised to find Rory there.

"Hey," Rory said, his dark eyes sweeping over the desk. "Malcolm already came down here? I knew there was a reason he sent Ty after me." He stepped inside, then closed the door behind himself but left it open a crack like he thought Samuel might launch across the desk and kiss him again. "Did he tell you?"

"About the historical society? Yeah, it's a great idea. I don't want to make a decision yet, though." He was surprised to hear himself say it, considering the time crunch, but it was the truth. Something was calcifying in his mind, something slowly becoming clear, but he wasn't sure yet and needed just a little more proof. "I want to talk it over at dinner."

"At dinner?" Rory echoed, brow furrowed. "With me?"

"Rory, don't tell me you've forgotten?" Samuel said in a mock offended tone, tilting his head to one side. "The world-famous Daniels Family Christmas Eve Eve Dinner?"

Rory gawked at him before putting his hand over his mouth, clearly stifling a laugh. The sheer warmth that shot through Samuel at the sight made something abundantly clear to him. He still loved Rory, had never really stopped, and he had to tell him before the chance had passed again. "Why am I invited?"

"Because my parents will literally go crazy if they don't get to see you while you're in town," Samuel said, shaking his head. "Come on. It's just going to be the family."

Rory's eyes softened, as easy to read as ever, clearly touched by the inclusion. "Okay. Malcolm is going to be working with Ty to get some pictures together for the historical society pitch, so he can't come. Is that okay?"

"Yes," Samuel said a little too quickly, something like amusement flashing across Rory's face, and Samuel got the distinct feeling that the other man hadn't been as bothered by being kissed as Samuel had thought. "I mean, if it's okay with you."

"It is," Rory said. "But first thing tomorrow we go to the society. I'm almost done with the paperwork."

"Already?" Samuel asked. "How?"

"I caught the president first thing this morning to get the paperwork," he said, shrugging one shoulder. "It's the right thing to do."

There was no way in hell Samuel was going to let Rory go again. If he had to be a homewrecker, so be it.

Chapter Nineteen

SNOW CRUNCHED under the tires of the rental car as Rory pulled off the main road onto the drive that led to the Danielses' bed and breakfast, a late-19th-century farmhouse that Samuel's grandfather had turned into the modern-day inn. Rory had made this drive hundreds of times before, although he had admittedly usually done it while half-asleep in the passenger seat of Samuel's truck. Tonight he was a bundle of nerves, though, the sight of the farmhouse with all its windows shining brightly unlocking a whole new level of guilt.

He had left Malcolm and Ty at the lodge, Ty methodically combing through hundreds of pictures he had taken to find the proper ones to include in the historical society proposal and Malcolm assisting, and while Rory was more confident of his plan than ever, he was also beginning to recognize a mounting pressure. The sensation had begun the night before when he had been kissed and had steadily increased over the course of the day, a growing conviction that he had to make a choice.

He knew even before Malcolm had pointed it out that the solution for the lodge was a career-killer. Strangely, that didn't bother him as much as it should have, which was, in turn, bothering him a lot. The way forward seemed clear and yet crushingly simple because he couldn't truly fathom it yet. He had spent his entire adolescence dreaming of escaping his hometown, but now he wanted nothing more than to return. He still loved Samuel, that much had been clear from his first impulsive lie, and the kiss, the way Samuel treated him, all pointed to his feelings being the same.

And yet he was uncertain. More than uncertain. Paralysis had overcome his decision-making, and he had the distinct feeling that he was careening toward a make-or-break moment.

He sighed, resisting the urge to smack his head against the steering wheel, and drove past the farmhouse down the side lane that led to the small two-story home where the Danielses actually lived.

Samuel's truck was parked at the bottom of the wooden steps that led up to a wraparound porch Rory had helped build the summer of his sophomore year. Rory parked alongside the truck, glancing at it to ensure it was empty before flipping down the sun visor and peering at himself in the mirror. Malcolm and Ty, who seemed both highly amused and slightly irritated by Rory's continued uncertainty, had assured him that he looked good, his curls tightly coiled and his beard and mustache well-groomed. Malcolm had lent him a deep green sweater, as nothing Rory had—aside from a garish vest he'd brought mostly because it seemed like he should have at least one Christmas item in his wardrobe—was appropriate for a Christmas dinner. Objectively, Rory knew he was handsome. He'd always been aware of his good looks, even as a teenager dyeing his hair blond to look edgy. Now, though, he couldn't decide if that was a good thing or not.

"Can't keep stalling," he muttered, pressing his palms to his eyes briefly before getting out of the car.

He hadn't even reached the bottom of the steps when the front door of the house flew open and Marion and Tim Daniels hurried out onto the porch, rushing down to meet him. Before Rory could even open his mouth, he was enveloped in a crushing hug, both older Danielses embracing him as though he'd never left. A surge of warmth rushed through Rory, a cascade of memories: Marion going out of her way to ensure Rory had a home-cooked meal more nights than not, Tim patiently teaching him and Samuel how to shave, the pair of them sitting at the dining room table and listening, accepting, as Rory and Samuel fumbled through coming out.

"You got so tall," Marion said, sniffling as she pulled back and peered up at him. "Oh, Rory, look at you!"

"A full-blown architect, huh?" Tim asked at the same time, and Rory could see that his hazel eyes were glistening with unshed tears as well. "We're so unbelievably proud of you."

"I'm so sorry" was all Rory could muster up, pulling them each into another hug in turn.

"Don't be ridiculous," Marion said, squeezing him so tightly he could burst. "You could have taken ninety years to come back and we'd still be so happy. Oh my God, I can't wait to hear about New York!"

"Are you guys going to let the poor man come inside?" Samuel was in the doorway now, arms crossed as light flooded out around him.

Rory had noticed it that morning, but there was a different air about Samuel, a definite sense of levity that hadn't been there earlier. "He's not used to this freezing weather anymore."

"Of course, of course," Marion said, and Rory was promptly pulled inside by both arms. It was as if he'd never left, immediately enveloped into the fold again despite his absence. Rory had forgotten, or perhaps forced himself to forget, how loved he had been by this family, but it was impossible for him to not remember now. The house was much the same, although Tim had remodeled the kitchen and gave Rory the grand tour as Samuel and Jasper set the table. Marion, who had filled her empty nest with a pair of ugly-yet-endearing dogs, showed Rory the tricks she had taught them and was so clearly pleased that Rory couldn't help but love them too.

Dinner itself was incredible. Rory wasn't a terrible cook, but he tended to meal prep and eat out more than he should. The clear love that had been imbued in every dish made everything taste ten times better, and the conversation was effortless, the entire family interested in what Rory had been doing and Rory just as interested in return. Even Jasper, who had seemed kind of moody when dinner had begun, was laughing and goofing off in no time. Rory couldn't remember the last time he had felt so at home.

"If I have one more bite I'll actually die," Samuel said, groaning as he stretched his arms above his head, Rory pointedly not looking at the small strip of skin exposed between his jeans and the bottom of his Christmas sweater. "Can we take a break before dessert?"

"For sure," Marion said, getting to her feet and beginning to clear dishes. Immediately everyone else rose to help her, and she laughed, waving her hands at them. "Go on, now. Tim and I will tidy up. It's not like there's a lot to do."

"Thanks, Grandma," Jasper said, immediately pulling out his phone and disappearing into the downstairs bathroom. Rory could put together the pieces and realize that, as preoccupied with Samuel as he was, Jasper was clearly the same in terms of Louis. Rory could also see that the Danielses were trying to manufacture a situation where he and Samuel could be alone, but he definitely wasn't ready for that yet. He needed to figure out what he was going to say.

"I'd like to wash my hands," he said before he could be cornered, looking around. "Is it okay if I use the bathroom upstairs?"

"Of course," Samuel said, and Rory had to convince himself he was wrong about the look on his face being one of disappointment. He headed upstairs, looking at the pictures lining the wall, touched to see that many of them included him even after all these years apart. Pictures of him and Samuel among a bloom of spring wildflowers, a day that had ended with Samuel sunburned and Rory bee-stung. Pictures of the entire family at the lake, the boys no more than ten and squinting against the sun, Jamie giving the camera a look of adolescent annoyance. Jamie's sixteenth birthday, Samuel and Rory roughhousing in the background. Surprisingly, there were a few pictures of just Rory, including the graduation one Jasper had told him about.

Heart aching, Rory reached the upstairs bathroom and washed his hands, so many thoughts tangling up in his mind that he genuinely didn't think he could make sense of them all. He had been avoiding the subject of Jamie, assuming that she had done the same thing he had and gotten the hell out of Evergreen as soon as she could, but now… now he felt like there was something looming, a thought at the back of his mind that he had been running from this entire time. He couldn't keep running, had to face this thing head-on or risk having nothing. He was half disappointed when he opened the bathroom door and found Samuel hadn't followed him upstairs, pausing in the hallway and glancing toward the stairs before turning the other way.

Samuel's old room—and by extension Rory's old room—was the second door on the left, and Rory opened it, stepped inside, and looked around. Aside from a couple spots where posters had peeled off the walls, it was entirely the same. Rory turned on the lamp that sat on the nightstand, settling on the edge of the bed and soaking up the nostalgia. There was a massive poster plastered to the ceiling that he and Samuel had stolen off the side of a building and painstakingly wallpapered to where it now was, a dozen or more T-shirts from various concerts, an entire wall covered in Polaroids and film photos, nearly every single one of them of him and Samuel.

"I figured you would end up here." Rory looked over to find Samuel in the doorway, looking around the room as well. "It's always weird to come in here, but my mom thinks it's cute, so she won't change it." His eyes settled on Rory, a slight smile tugging at his lips. "Do you have a minute to talk?"

"I don't want you to say anything for a minute," Rory said, still afraid but no longer capable of running. "Just come sit down."

Samuel did as he was told, Rory flopping on his back on the bed the moment Samuel sat, and neither of them said anything for a few long moments before Rory spoke. "When I left, I was upset and I was angry, but more than anything else, I knew that I never wanted to be in the position where I could have my heart broken again. So I made sure I never was. I dated, but I never let it get too serious, and I never brought down the cage I'd put up around my heart. I just knew that if I let anyone in again, if I allowed them anywhere near my heart, I was opening myself up to being heartbroken all over again."

He paused, taking a deep breath before continuing. "But I think that was just an excuse, honestly. I think deep down I always figured I would somehow find you again. That whatever had kept us apart would be fixed at some point. I know I bear a huge chunk of the responsibility. I cut you out and never even tried to figure out why you didn't follow. And the more time that passed, the more I became convinced that the right thing to do was to stay away. I wasn't even going to look you up while I was in town. If I hadn't seen you at the lodge, we wouldn't be sitting here right now."

"Rory—"

"No, hold on," Rory said, turning his head to avoid Samuel's gaze still. "I was so hellbent on staying out of your life that when I saw Jasper and I saw that ring on your finger…. The only thing I could think was that if you were married with a kid, then I couldn't fathom the thought of looking like I had been sitting around waiting for you all these years. I didn't even know it yet, but that was exactly what I was doing, and the idea of having you realize it made me want to die."

He'd come to the crux of it now, the truth of what he'd done, and he covered his face with his hands to shield himself from what was coming. "I lied to you, Sam. God, I lied like such an asshole. I came in that first day and I told you to your face that Malcolm was my fiancé, but he's not. He's just my coworker, and he agreed to lie because I promised I'd let him make partner ahead of me, but I'm a fucking idiot and you weren't even married and—"

"Rory." Samuel's voice came from directly above him, and Rory peered through his fingers to find Samuel leaning over him, face only a few inches away. Instead of looking angry or disappointed, he was visibly amused, a smirk twitching at the side of his mouth. "Can you please let me talk now?"

Rory stared at him, incapable of speaking, and Samuel took his silence as a tacit agreement to begin. "Do you remember when that skinhead came after us at that metal show in Buffalo?"

"Yeah," Rory said, removing his hands fully from his face. Samuel was still looking down at him, and framed against the ancient ceiling poster, he was impossibly handsome. "Why?"

"Because the minute you thought we were in trouble, you told the guy we were half-brothers. For the rest of the night, you just totally kept up the act. Refused to hold my hand, wouldn't kiss me, the whole shebang. I was so pissed at the end of the night, and when we got back to the truck, I was ready to get in the biggest fight. And before I could do shit, you kissed me like you'd been waiting ages to get to, and when I asked you why you lied to that guy, you acted so confused and said you didn't want to cause any trouble for me. Like I was the only thing that mattered."

"You were," Rory said. "I didn't want to even imagine you getting hurt because you were with me."

"But you took that all on yourself, Rory. Do you get what I'm saying?"

Rory stared up at him, realization hitting him like a piano dropped from a crane. He'd done the same damn thing here, had assumed that his presence in Samuel's life would cause him more difficulties than anything else, and he'd plunged into a lie without even stopping to consider the fallout. He could see in Samuel's eyes that they had finally reached the same page. "Sam—"

Samuel's hand settled against Rory's throat, his fingers warm and calloused against the stubble of Rory's beard, and he leaned down to meet Rory where he lay, then kissed him deeply and without hesitation. This time Rory kissed back, a relief flooding him that seemed entirely impossible after the mistakes he had made. Samuel was kissing him hungrily, thumb caressing Rory's jaw in slow, sweeping strokes, lips parted enough for Rory to drag his tongue along Samuel's in a slick and long-missed movement.

The sound of a throat being cleared came from the direction of the doorway, and Samuel and Rory pulled apart, Rory certain he looked as disheveled as his thoughts currently were. Jasper was standing there, grinning like he'd just stumbled into the most amusing thing he'd ever seen. "Grandma says dessert is ready," he said innocently. "Do you want me to close the door so you two can keep going?"

Samuel launched one of the pillows sitting on the bed at his son, who caught it, laughing. "Brat," he said. "We'll be right down. Don't tell your grandparents we were kissing, or I'll tell them about your vape, got it?"

Jasper yelped, clearly playing along with the threat, and tossed the pillow back at his dad before heading down the hallway toward the stairs. Samuel groaned, dropping the pillow back on the bed before smiling down at Rory, his eyes crinkling endearingly. "We've been busted," he said, flopping on his back.

"We should go down, shouldn't we?" Rory asked, rolling onto his side, and Samuel looked at him.

"Give me five minutes to think about calculus and naked old women," Samuel said, grinning. "I don't think I should go down in my current state."

Rory stared at him blankly for a moment before it clicked, and he smacked Samuel on the arm, laughing harder than he had in a while. "Pervert," he said, but he didn't think he could recall a time he'd been so light, so happy.

Chapter Twenty

"ARE THEY coming?" Marion asked, and it took literally every molecule of self-control Jasper possessed not to make a dirty joke in front of his grandmother. He still couldn't quite believe what he had seen, except that he had definitely seen it. His dad and Rory making out hadn't been in his cards for the night, but it filled him with a strange sort of hope that they had figured things out. He'd been in a shitty mood all day, unable to get Louis's attention except for some terse text messages, but this had turned his attitude around.

"Yeah, they should be down in a sec," Jasper said, helping Marion carry dessert—an apple pie and whipped cream—to the table. A floorboard creaked overhead, signaling that his dad and Rory had managed to extricate themselves, and he looked at his grandmother with wide eyes. "They were kissing," he whispered, and Marion grinned at the news.

"Is that so?" she asked, beginning to set out the dessert plates. "Well now, those two always did struggle with keeping that door closed. Your poor grandfather was always the first one up in the morning, and he must have caught them half a dozen times."

"Gross," Jasper said.

"What's gross?" Samuel asked as he entered the room, practically glowing with obvious pleasure, Rory trailing after him.

"You two kissing," Jasper said, only to burst into a fit of laughter as Samuel manhandled him into his arms, covering his mouth. Despite a recent growth spurt that had left Jasper taller, he readily allowed his dad to roughhouse him, only to go limp in an attempt to drag Samuel to the ground.

"Boys, please!" Marion said, laughing as Tim came into the kitchen, having taken the break between dinner and dessert to check on the bed and breakfast. "Tim, can you please control them?"

"If I knew how to do that, I'd have started years ago," Tim said, sounding long-suffering but tipping Rory a wink as he took off his winter coat. "Why are they fighting?"

"Dad and Rory kissed!" Jasper announced from his spot on the floor, Samuel crouched beside him, panting from the exertion of getting his son on the ground.

"Just like old times, then," Tim teased gently, Rory glad his blush wasn't visible. "Come on, leave your poor father alone. I'm ready for pie."

Jasper clambered to his feet, pulling Samuel up after him, and the family settled around the table. Honestly, Jasper couldn't stop thinking about what had happened, although he was selfishly framing it in terms of his own feelings. If Rory could figure things out with his father and admit he'd lied about Malcolm, Jasper could fix things with Louis. He knew he could, the prospect of giving up on something he truly wanted more than he could bear. "Can I take the truck? I think I'm going to skip dessert," he said, looking at his dad.

"Why?" Samuel asked, surprised out of the conversation he and Rory were having with Tim about the plan for the lodge. "We drove down together."

"I want to catch Louis before he goes to bed," Jasper admitted, glancing at Rory briefly. "I think I should talk to him face-to-face."

"Oh, well, I was going to drive Rory—"

"You can take the rental car, if that's okay with your dad," Rory said, digging the keys out of his pocket. "Just give the keys to Malcolm or Ty if you see them."

"Are they together?" Samuel asked, his tone making it clear he hadn't even remotely considered the possibility before that moment.

"Yes," Jasper and Rory said in unison, Samuel clearly stunned.

"Can I go, Dad?" Jasper asked, unsure even as he took the keys from Rory.

"You can, but you need to drive a hundred times more carefully than usual," Samuel said. "Got it?"

"Got it," Jasper said, hopping to his feet.

"I'll come grab my wallet," Rory said, getting up as well. He waited for Jasper to say his goodbyes before following him out front, stopping at the trunk of the car, and looking at Jasper. "Are you going to make up with him?"

"I'm gonna try," Jasper said, determined. "If you guys can make up after twenty years, then I can figure things out with Louis. That's all I want to do right now."

"I don't know how good my advice is, but just be honest with him," Rory said, an earnest note to his voice that hadn't been there before. "I don't know how he did it, but your dad managed to figure it out before I could even tell him. All l could think was that I wanted him to know the truth before it was too late."

Jasper looked at him, filled with an affection for Rory that genuinely surprised him. "Did you really make up with my dad?"

"I think we need to have a conversation to clear some stuff up, but I'm not going to run away this time," Rory said, sounding sure of himself. "Did you tell him about Malcolm?"

"No, I honestly think he figured it out himself," Jasper said, seeming just as surprised as Rory. "I think Malcolm and Ty got to the point where they were being too obvious for even him to ignore."

"Go and fix things with Louis," Rory said, patting him on the shoulder. "I hope you know it's something worth fixing."

"Thanks," Jasper said, grinning at Rory before getting into the rental car. He watched Rory head back to the house and waited a few more seconds to steel his nerves before beginning the short drive up to the lodge. He'd been fixated on repairing things with Louis since the night prior, but in the time apart, he'd made a discovery that felt both impulsive and right. He needed to wait for the dust to settle, for the lodge to be safe, before he could really tell anyone, but Louis was different.

Upon reaching the lodge he found Malcolm and Ty occupying their usual spot in the lobby, the coffee table set up in front of the couch plastered in documents and pictures. As Jasper approached he found they were engaged in a heated debate over whether or not the 1920s addition to the lodge in the restaurant was considered true art deco, but Malcolm sounded like he was genuinely enjoying the argument. "Hey," Jasper said, holding the rental car keys out to Malcolm. "Have you seen Louis?"

"Why do you have Rory's keys?" Malcolm asked, taking them nonetheless. "Didn't you have dinner tonight?"

"Yeah, but Rory and my dad won't stop making out, so I left," Jasper said, giving his words a moment to sink in and grinning as the pair both looked at him in surprise. "Apparently my dad figured out Rory was lying. Not really sure how he managed to do that considering how clueless he usually is, but…."

"Oh, that could possibly be because I called him stupid this morning and told him I would burn down the lodge if he didn't smarten up," Malcolm said, shrugging one shoulder. "You'll be pleased to know that the information Rory asked Ty and I to get together is almost done. The historical society will have a hell of a time refusing his proposal tomorrow."

"Good," Jasper said, the news redoubling his determination to find Louis. "Have you guys seen Louis? I need to talk to him."

"I'm pretty sure he's having dinner with his parents in the restaurant," Ty offered. "Do you know if your dad kept the original balustrades for the stairs, by the way?"

"No, sorry," Jasper said, already backing away, and not really sure what a balustrade was. "Thanks for the tip! Sorry about what I did to the rental car, Malcolm!" With that final joke—the car was perfectly fine— Jasper turned and headed for the restaurant. He found Louis sitting at a table with his parents, dark circles under his eyes and his skin paler than usual. Maybe this whole thing was eating Louis up just as much as it was eating at Jasper.

"Hey," he said, catching a passing waiter by the arm. "Can you ask the guy at table twelve to come over here?"

"Yeah, man," the waiter said, making a beeline to the table. Jasper watched the waiter speaking to Louis, Louis looking in his direction briefly before seeming to make a split-second decision and getting to his feet. The look on his face was one of clear irritation, but Jasper had been prepared for it, was ready to undo the damage.

"What do you want?" Louis asked once he was in earshot, crossing his arms and looking at Jasper. "Is having dinner with my parents a symbol of me being a traitor? Are you going to scold me some more?"

"No," Jasper said, taking the accusations in stride. "Can you give me ten minutes before you decide you hate me?"

"Why?" Louis asked, clearly unconvinced. "That ship has sailed."

"I don't think that's true," he said. "Come on, follow me. Please."

Thankfully, Louis allowed him at least that much and followed him out of the restaurant and down the same side hall where Jasper and Rory had spoken the night before. Out of the bustle and din of the rest of the lodge, Jasper turned and looked at Louis. "I was out of line last night," he said, as plaintive as he could be. "I panicked at the idea of losing my house, and I took it out on you in the heat of the moment, and it's not an excuse, but it is the truth. And you would be well within your rights to not want anything to do with me, but the fact is that I want everything to do with you. I want go to NYU and date you and figure out how to fall in love with you because I think with time we would get there. That's it. I like you more than I've liked anyone before, and that's it."

Louis looked at him, narrowing his eyes with some trepidation, his arms still crossed. "You really hurt my feelings last night," he finally said. "You know I'm not some pawn of my dad, right? I think what he's doing is fucked up, and I'm not interested in helping him with it. I went on a date with you because I wanted to. How do I know that you won't suspect me of not being sincere again?"

"You don't, except that I'm telling you I won't," Jasper said. "You guys are here until the New Year, right?"

"Yeah," Louis said, letting his arms drop to his sides. "What do you actually want?"

"All I want is a chance," Jasper said. "Look, I've spent the last two weeks watching my dad dance around the fact that he's still in love with Rory. I don't want to reach that point. You can't seriously tell me you haven't thought the same thing."

Louis sighed, not looking Jasper in the eyes, but his shoulders slumped a little despite his clear attempts to keep himself on guard. "I don't think you and me making out on Christmas vacation is the same caliber as your dad and Rory, honestly."

"Well, no, but what if we regret it just because I'm an idiot?" Jasper asked. "All I want is to make sure that you and I don't miss an opportunity here. I think we're compatible, and I want to give it a shot."

There was a brief silence before Louis groaned, reaching out and gripping Jasper's shirt with both hands. He shook him slightly, his frustration obvious. "What do you want me to say?" he asked, frowning at Jasper. "I like you, okay? I think you're hot and funny, and you're easy to spend time with, but you really pissed me off last night. Do you know how hard it is for me to make friends? We're constantly moving, and when you said you were planning on going to NYU, I thought it would be nice to have you. But you fucking pigeonholed me as some rich kid under his daddy's thumb and literally pissed me off so bad. I don't want to give you another chance."

"What if I say sorry again?" Jasper asked, gripping Louis's wrists and flexing his fingers against his skin. "What if I say sorry every day until you leave in the New Year, and then I text you every single day until

September? Would that be enough for you to forgive me? Because I'm dead serious about you, Louis. I'd like to know you better, and I really think we could be a cute couple and—"

He was prevented from saying more by Louis yanking him forward, kissing him so hard on the mouth Jasper was almost positive he could taste blood. Startled, Jasper began to kiss back, although Louis broke off the kiss before he could truly get into it. "Shut up," he said, shaking Jasper again. "Why are you being so goddamn stubborn about this?"

"Because I messed up and want to fix it," Jasper said, rubbing at his lip and finding that it was split. "I wasn't lying when I said that I like you and want to try and date you, if you'd let me. If you tell me to my face that you think we shouldn't give it another shot, I'll give it up, but I don't think you will."

Louis groaned, dropping his head against Jasper's collarbone. "If anyone else had accused me of being some kind of honeypot for my dad I would have no fucking problem cutting them out, but I don't want to cut you out. I can't stop thinking about it, and I just… you know, I feel like I messed up too. You hurt my feelings a lot, but I think, uh… I don't know. I think I overreacted too. I don't get it, but… I'm sorry too. I am."

"I think we both overreacted," Jasper murmured. "But I think at the end of it, we both like each other. And I think that might be enough, if we want it to be."

Louis lifted his head, not looking entirely convinced but narrowing his eyes in a way that no longer seemed angry but rather slightly irritated. Jasper, still holding Louis's wrists, pulled him closer and kissed him again, and this time Louis didn't pull away after only a few brief moments.

Chapter Twenty-One

"WHERE, UH, are we going?" Rory peered out of the passenger window of the truck, Samuel driving them deeper and deeper into the property behind the farmhouse, entirely off-road through the snow that coated the ground, more fat and fluffy flakes falling softly as they went. As kids, he and Samuel had explored every inch of the Danielses' property, the woods and rolling terrain a source of endless fascination for a pair of boys who had read *Lord of the Rings* a million times. At this time of night, though, it was hard to tell where they were headed.

"Wow," Samuel said, mock-disappointed. "You've forgotten more than I thought, Rory. It's sad."

"Shut up," Rory said, punching Samuel lightly on the arm. "We never used to drive out here, even as kids."

"No, you're right. Do you remember when we schlepped all the camping stuff out here and I got heat stroke so bad I threw up all night?"

"Ugh, yes, and you kept letting every mosquito in a sixty-mile radius into the tent? By morning I looked like I'd rolled in poison ivy, and you looked like a dehydrated husk. I was so scared we were going to turn into an urban legend about two kids who'd gone missing in the backwoods of Vermont."

Samuel laughed, deftly maneuvering the truck up between a pair of stately oak trees and onto a flat and treeless plateau. Samuel stopped the truck after a couple moments more of crunching through the snow, put it in park but let the engine idle. "Okay, give me a second to get things set up," Samuel said, hopping out of the truck before Rory could ask what exactly he was setting up.

God, he was happy. Not just happy, but content in a way that he didn't think he had been in decades. He knew he and Samuel needed to talk, to have a serious conversation about where this left them, but he was so pleased that Samuel hadn't immediately rejected him upon hearing that he'd lied that he had confidence they could figure anything out now. It seemed so obvious to Rory that he had been waiting for this moment for years, that finding his way back to Samuel had always been in his subconscious. He wasn't sure if he believed in soulmates, but twenty years had not dampened how he felt about Samuel in the slightest.

Rory was pulled out of his reverie by the sharp rap of knuckles against the passenger window. "It's ready," Samuel said, voice muffled before he opened the door. "Sorry, it's ready."

Rory got out of the truck, glad he'd remembered both a hat and gloves before leaving the lodge earlier, and looked up at Samuel. "What's ready?"

"Our date, of course," Samuel said, grabbing Rory's hand and pulling him around to the bed of the truck. Rory, who really hadn't paid much attention to the truck at all even when he'd been in it before, saw now that what he had assumed was a tarp over the back of the truck had, in fact, been a collapsed tent. Samuel had popped the tent into place and grinned at Rory, helping him climb into the bed before clambering in after him.

The bed was full of blankets, to the point where Rory suspected Samuel had stolen every last textile from his parents' house, and as Rory settled into the nest Samuel had built, he realized that there was a bottle of wine, two glasses, and a Tupperware container of apple pie. "Oh my God," he said, laughing as he watched Samuel flop down next to him, bumping their knees together. "What is this? How did you even manage to pull this off?"

"I got my mom to distract you after you came back in from talking to Jasper," Samuel said. "Why do you think she was suddenly so interested in the architectural design of skyscrapers?"

"The oldest trick in the book," Rory said, drawing his legs up toward him to tuck his knees against his chest and resting his cheek on one of them so he could look at Samuel. "This is really cute, Sam. Thank you."

"Don't get too excited," Samuel said, unscrewing the cap of the wine bottle. "I only have the cheap stuff."

"I'm fine with that," Rory said, shifting so he could hold the glasses for Samuel. Honestly, Samuel could give him swamp water at this point and he would be happy. The truck bed was poorly lit by a camping lantern, and yet Samuel looked model-handsome, taking a sip of the red wine and pulling an exaggerated face. "You're still the most handsome guy I've ever seen, you know."

"Really?" Samuel asked, looking over at him. "You've seen Malcolm, right?"

"Malcolm's too pretty," Rory said, shaking his head. "No, you've always been my type." He took a drink as well, the wine a bit too sweet but still pleasant. "I missed you. Even being back here made me feel like I was crawling out of my skin to get back to you despite not having the guts to do anything about it."

"You had the guts. You just thought I was married." Samuel fiddled with the ring on his left hand, glancing over at Rory. "I think I'm ready to tell you everything. Why I didn't come after you."

"You don't have to, if it's too much," Rory said. He was curious, but that meant little in the grand scheme of things. His trust in Samuel was restored to full confidence.

"No, I think you should know," Samuel said, drumming his fingers against the side of the glass as he thought. "I got up that morning to go and see you off. I wasn't going to just let you leave without an explanation. I knew maybe you'd be pissed I wasn't coming with you, but I was going to promise to visit, and I knew you'd understand. I was getting dressed, and I guess Jamie heard me awake because she came in my room crying."

Rory listened, suspicions that had been fomenting since he had spoken with Ty the other night beginning to take a more concrete shape. Jamie would have been twenty-one the summer he'd left, a graphic design student at community college who worked at the bed and breakfast on the weekends, and while Rory had been close with her, he had also assumed she had been off living her own life outside of Evergreen Hill. It was seeming more and more likely that all his assumptions since arriving back in town had been entirely incorrect.

"I think she forgot you were leaving that morning," Samuel continued. "Or she had worked herself up so badly she just didn't realize what was going on. But, uh, do you remember her boyfriend back then?"

"Yeah, ugh, what did we call him?" Rory asked, struggling to remember. "Frankie, right? And we called him Frankie Valli because he went through that weird greaser phase, didn't he?"

"Yes, bingo!" Samuel said, enthusiastically smacking Rory's thigh in the process. "Okay, so Jamie comes in just sobbing, and I'd been crying since I got up, but I dried it up really fast because she freaked me out, and she is so upset she can barely talk. Finally she tells me that, like, a month and a half ago, she and Frank were having sex, and the condom broke. And now she's almost two weeks late and can I please go get a pregnancy test because Frank's brother works at the pharmacy and he'll tell Frank."

Samuel took a deep breath, this story clearly one he had been dying to tell Rory for years. "I figured, you know, that I could pick up the test for her and still have time to catch you at the station. I didn't really want to, I wanted to see you, but Jamie was so hysterical that I knew I couldn't just leave her like that. I went and picked up the test for her and got home pretty quickly, but…."

"It was positive," Rory murmured, taking another sip of wine and shifting so he could rest his head on Samuel's shoulder. "Oh, Sam."

"I couldn't leave her alone that morning. She was so upset, and no one else was awake, and… I just missed my chance to get to you." Samuel said like he was apologizing, tilting his head so his cheek was resting against Rory's curls. "And I missed saying goodbye. I thought you would call when you got to the city, but you never did, and I just… I just let you go. Mom and Dad's friends at the cafe said you were settling in well, so I just figured you didn't want anything to do with me, and by the time I thought it might not be true, it was too late to reach out."

Rory was quiet, knowing precisely what Samuel meant because it had been the same thing that had happened to him. He'd been angry and heartbroken when he'd reached New York, and by the time those emotions had dulled and reason had prevailed, he had felt it was too late to reach out. "And Jasper?"

"He was born at the end of March after you left. A little bit premature, but he did well, and both Jamie and Frank were as happy as could be." He sighed softly, breath ghosting over Rory's hair and forehead. "I was babysitting him one day when he was about eleven months old. I'd gotten a job working the front desk at the lodge, and they let me bring Jasper with me if he stayed in a chest carrier. Jamie and Frank had gone down to Montpelier to get some shopping done and pick up a used stroller for Jas and, well…. They hit a patch of black ice on the way back. They were killed instantly. My parents talked about adopting Jasper, but I was his godfather, and I loved him more than anything, so I did it instead, and there's never been a day where I'm not glad I did."

Rory had noticed Jamie's absence but had never once thought she was dead, even after he'd begun to suspect she was Jasper's true parent. He'd never asked because he'd never assumed it would be something as awful as death, that any explanations of her absence could wait. Jamie had been bright and motivated, and Rory had figured she was off somewhere far more interesting than here. That Samuel had spent the last twenty years carrying the burden of losing his sister and raising her son.... "I never would have left you alone if I had known," he said. "If I'd heard what had happened...."

"I've been thinking a lot about that since you came back," Samuel said, raising his hand to curl his fingers against Rory's cheek. "About the kind of person you would be now if you had given up on your dream to stay here with me. And on the flipside, what kind of person I would be if I had you here to lean on. For years I thought my life would be better if you had stayed, but seeing who you are now has made it clear as anything that our lives wouldn't have been better, they just would have been different. In any case, there was never anyone else for me."

"You didn't go on any dates?" Rory teased, Samuel laughing. "I went on dates. Had a couple boyfriends too, but they never stuck."

"I went on some dates too, but I never really hit it off with anyone. Being a bisexual single father in a town this small didn't do me any favors in the dating scene at all."

"Bisexual!" Rory exclaimed, pulling away so he could look at Samuel. "You've been dating women behind my back?"

Samuel laughed, finishing off his wine before pouring a little more and topping off Rory's for him as well. "Not very successfully. I think most women in town can't forget how glued to the hip you and I were."

"Well, I don't care," Rory said, wedging his wine between his thighs so he could grip Samuel's face and kiss him on the tip of his nose. "I don't care if I'm the only man you've ever found attractive, because after tonight you're never going to need to go on another date." He kissed Samuel on the apple of his cheek and then his jaw, drawing him closer with each kiss.

"What if it's a date with you?" Samuel murmured, chuckling softly as he was kissed repeatedly. "Is that acceptable?"

"Hm," Rory hummed as though he was actually uncertain, looking into Samuel's hazel eyes made that much darker by the dim light. "Maybe that's acceptable. Is tonight a date?"

"I think so," Samuel said. He stole another kiss from Rory before searching his face closely. "What about New York?"

"Leave that to me," Rory said, sounding confident. "It'll be figured out by Christmas."

"Are you going to stay?"

"Don't worry about that tonight," Rory said, kissing him again on the mouth. "I know you and I aren't going to be separated again, not if I have anything to say about it."

"Is that so?" Samuel asked, a huskiness in his voice that sent a thrill through Rory. He drained his glass of wine and set it aside, Rory strangely tickled by his unwillingness to spill it even while trying to be seductive. He couldn't help but snort, Samuel grinning at him. "What?"

"I just can't believe how different you are but how little you've changed," Rory said, pulling him into another kiss. "I really don't know how I didn't realize immediately that I was still in love with you."

"Oh, you're still in love with me?" Samuel asked, grimacing even as he freed the wineglass from between Rory's thighs and set it aside. "That's embarrassing. I just lured you out here to make out with you."

"You're not doing a very good job of it," Rory said, hauling a leg over Samuel's lap so he was straddling him and pushing his thumbs against Samuel's jaw to force his head back. "I've barely been made out with at all."

"Well, let's rectify that," Samuel murmured, resting one broad hand on Rory's waist and the other on the back of his head, pulling him down into a deep, hungry kiss, the actions of a man who had been starving for so long and had now come across a feast.

Rory was only too happy to oblige.

Chapter Twenty-Two

RORY GROANED, vaguely aware of a pain in his lower back and a weight on his legs, topped off by the steady vibration of a phone somewhere nearby. Mouth dry and everything feeling faintly sticky, Rory managed to get himself into a sitting position, finding that the weight on him was Samuel, softly snoring and cocooned in most of the blankets alongside Rory. Struck with sudden affection, Rory pushed his fingers back through Samuel's thick hair, the memories of the night before oozing back in with welcome clarity.

No wonder his back hurt. Sex in the bed of a truck was nothing new when it came to his relationship with Samuel, their teenage years an exercise in figuring out how to avoid parental supervision, but he was nearly forty now and hadn't had sex in over a year to boot. Still…. Sex with Samuel was unlike anything else he had ever experienced.

The vibration stopped before starting again, and Rory looked around until he found his phone shoved far down under the blankets in the back of the truck. He had four missed calls from Malcolm and a fifth ringing now, and Rory managed to answer it, voice sleep-thick. "What's going on?"

"Oh my God," Malcolm said, and even without seeing him Rory knew he was pinching the bridge of his nose. "Do you have any idea what time it is?"

Rory pulled his phone away from his ear, looked at the time, and felt his heart sink. "Nine forty-five?" he said in disbelief to Malcolm. "How is that possible?"

"You need to be at the historical society in fifteen minutes. Me and Ty will meet you down there with your notes and the pictures, but you need to get a move on."

"Wait, before you hang up," Rory said, Malcolm huffing into the receiver. "Can you bring me a change of clothes? Uh… including underwear."

A heavy silence before Malcolm huffed again, Rory imagining him rubbing his forehead in frustration. "Yes, fine. Be there on time, Rory, or you're literally wasting everyone's time."

"Got it," Rory said, hanging up and leaning back over Samuel. This time instead of playing with Samuel's hair he shook his shoulder gently, already digging around for the keys. "Samuel," he said, receiving a groan in return. "We're going to miss the meeting I set with the historical society."

"Historical society?" Samuel repeated, sitting up slightly. Rory had to force himself to not get distracted by the clear hickey he'd left on Samuel's left pec. "You made a meeting with them already?"

"Yes, and it's in fifteen minutes," Rory said, fishing around for his jeans and finding them inside out in one of the blankets. "God, did you rip my clothes off or what?"

"Rory, hold on," Samuel said, voice muffled by the sweater he was pulling on over his head. "Malcolm told me everything yesterday morning."

"About the proposal, right?" Rory asked, bracing himself against the cab of the truck so he could yank his jeans on. "I know, you told me."

"No, he told me this is risking your job," Samuel said, finding his own pants and beginning to tug them on. He looked up to find Rory looking at him, eyes narrowed slightly. "What?"

"Nothing, let's talk and drive," Rory said, shrugging on a coat to cover his bare chest. "Quick, come on!"

Thankfully it took only a few seconds for Samuel to collapse the tent so they could drive, the truck cutting easily through the snow despite the fresh coat that had fallen overnight. They hadn't made it far before Samuel turned the radio down nearly all the way. "Tell me. No more lies, Rory."

"It's not a lie," Rory said, tilting his head so he could look at Samuel. "I told you last night to leave things to me." He smiled, visibly tired but pleased all the same. "Give me an hour, okay? One hour and everything will fall into place."

"Hm," Samuel said. "I don't know, you seem like a liar now. How am I supposed to trust you?"

"Shut up," Rory said, groaning. "I already told you why I lied."

"Yeah, to make me jealous," Samuel said, but he reached across the center console to grip Rory's hand nonetheless. Despite the danger posed by Samuel not having both hands on the wheel, Rory's heart gave an unruly flutter. He hadn't felt so young, so foolhardy, in years, and he tangled his fingers with Samuel's as they made their quiet way downtown.

THEY REACHED the historical society with three minutes to spare, and both Malcolm and Ty seemed to appear out of nowhere, Rory scrambling out to meet them. Malcolm shoved a bag into Rory's hands, and with Samuel holding the tent roof up enough for Rory to change, he managed to get dressed in clothes that didn't smell of sweat and spilled wine. "You owe me," Malcolm said as he handed over Rory's laptop, Ty holding out an envelope containing the application along with a dozen or so photographs.

"Don't worry, this will fix everything," Rory said, starting for the door of the society before turning back and pulling Samuel down into a brief but intense kiss. "One hour, got it?" he asked as he drew away, poking Samuel in the chest before turning and heading into the building.

As soon as the door had closed behind him, Ty turned to Samuel, grinning. "Mystery solved, huh?"

"What mystery?" Samuel asked, touching his lips gently and tearing his gaze away from where Rory had gone to look at Malcolm and Ty. "Nothing happened."

"Yeah, yeah," Ty said, but he took Malcolm's hand in his own as if he had been waiting to confirm if Samuel was aware of the lie Rory had told before showing any true affection. "Any objections to grabbing coffee while we wait?"

Samuel had to admit that now he knew Rory and Malcolm weren't together he was much more inclined to like Malcolm. The guy was far from a dick, although he had a dry sense of humor that took some getting used to, made worse by the faint Scottish accent he clearly hadn't been able to shake yet. He was also visibly besotted with Ty, often staring at the photographer while mid-conversation like he couldn't get enough of what he was seeing.

The hour seemed to drag on endlessly, Samuel drinking so much coffee his leg seemed doomed to bounce forever as a result, and while Malcolm and Ty gave him a rundown of the presentation, it seemed impossible that it would work, much less result in the negation of the injunction.

Around fifteen minutes before the hour was up Jasper appeared, face pink from the chill outside. While he was alone—and admitted he had bullied Clark into letting him take one of the lodge's shuttle buses to get into town—his mood was so markedly different from the night before that Samuel knew he'd fixed whatever misunderstanding he'd had with Louis. "I can't believe you guys made it," Jasper said, sitting in the booth alongside his father after picking up his coffee from the bar. "I thought Malcolm was going to have an aneurysm when Rory wouldn't pick up his phone."

"I just didn't want to give the presentation myself," Malcolm said, resting his arm on the back of the booth behind Ty, the pair of them settled across the table from Samuel and Jasper. "Rory said he'd take any blame that came my way for helping with the research, but I don't think I'd be so easily absolved if I actually did the convincing."

"What is his argument, actually?" Jasper asked, tone thoughtful. "Can the lodge actually be declared a historical building?"

"I think the odds are fairly good," Malcolm said. "The lodge is old enough to be considered a historical relic, and the story of the first owner is compelling. The only detracting factors we could find were some renovations the previous owners did in the eighties or nineties that would need to be reversed to bring it in line with the historical record, but Rory could sell anything to anyone." He snorted, lip twitching in the slightest amusement. "Hell, he convinced me to pretend to be his boyfriend, didn't he?"

"Why did you agree?" Samuel asked, curious. "And, uh.... Why did you kiss him?"

"Because we were sent here as part of a competition to make partner at our firm," Malcolm said. "And he offered to drop out if I helped him convince you that he hadn't been pining over you for the better part of twenty years." Malcolm looked at him, pale eyes clearly teasing. "And I kissed him to see if it would speed things up."

"If I ever become this sort of adult, please kill me," Jasper said, ducking as his father reached over to playfully cuff his ears. "Oh, shit, look," he said, sitting back up quickly. "Rory's out."

They all turned to watch as Rory crossed the street, no longer holding the envelope but keeping his laptop underneath his arm. He clearly realized the only place they could have gone was the cafe because he pushed inside, after stopping just briefly to knock the snow off his boots, then spotted them and came over. "Scooch, Jas," he said, pressing into the booth alongside the teenager. Despite the relative bulk of both Daniels men, they squished over even further, Rory sighing as soon as he was sitting down.

Samuel reached out to grip the nape of Rory's neck, but his fingers brushed against the collar of his shirt, and he frowned. "Rory."

"I know, I know, hold on," Rory said, closing his eyes. "There's so much that happened."

"No, it's not that. Your sweater is inside out."

"What?" Rory's eyes popped open again, and he groped at the back of his neck, groaning. "Oh my God! No wonder that lady kept rubbing her neck when she was looking at me! I thought she was having an allergic reaction or something."

"Are we going to lose the lodge because you couldn't dress yourself this morning?" Jasper asked, and Rory elbowed him gently.

"No, I didn't lose the lodge," Rory said. "Not even close." He grinned, the tension that had been at the table since he'd arrived easing somewhat as he relaxed, although he was clearly tired. "The society agreed that our proposal was sound. The lodge will be ratified before the New Year as the most recent addition to historical buildings in this county, and the president is going to talk to a municipal judge." He looked around, shrugging one shoulder, but he was obviously pleased. "Basically they want to make sure that the injunction can be blocked and the land transfer ratified the way it should have been in the 1900s."

"This all sounds too good to be true," Samuel said. "What's the catch?"

"Well," Rory said, looking at him before glancing down. "That's the thing. The lodge isn't in line with the society's current standards for historical buildings because of some of the aesthetic renovations done before you bought it." He opened his laptop, pulling up a digital blueprint he'd created to pinpoint the areas. "Mostly these changes were made to the outer facade and the lobby, but the work required to undo them and restore the original carpentry is intense. The society has agreed to give you a year of leeway to make these changes, and if they aren't completed, then at that point the injunction will come into play again."

Panic flashed in Samuel's eyes, and Rory raised his hand, cutting off his protest before he could voice it. "Look," he said, rubbing at his jaw. "Doing this today has jeopardized my job with the firm, but that isn't the part that scares me."

"Just tell him the plan, Rory," Malcom said, then finished his coffee.

Rory shot Malcolm a dirty look before sighing and looking at Samuel, Jasper leaning back to give him unfettered access. "You don't have to move, Jas," Rory said. "Sam, the truth is that when Malcolm and I came up with this plan, we realized it wasn't exactly something you could do on your own. The process of properly restoring a building like the lodge is grueling even without a time limit, and the society recognizes that. They were, uh… unwilling to agree to adding you to the register if you were going to take on those renovations alone."

Samuel felt his heart sink, his relief at the news now replaced by a growing anxiety. Rory could see this change and put up his hands. "We had planned for this, though. But I think I was being presumptuous."

He took a deep breath, finally at the crux of the issue. "I told the society I had made the decision to retire from my position in New York in order to head up the work on the lodge. Malcolm and I developed a twelve-month plan for renovations, and Ty took pictures of the problem areas, and the society is satisfied with that proposal."

Both Samuel and Jasper were staring at him now, near identical hazel eyes fixed on him in disbelief. Samuel was the first one to come to his senses, his voice quiet. "Are you saying what I think you're saying?"

"I don't want you to lose the lodge," Rory said, feeling himself blush, heat creeping up the back of his neck. "But I think I…." He paused, shaking his head. "I don't know. Going to New York made me who I am, but I've been getting the feeling that Evergreen Hill is where I'm meant to be again." He didn't add the most pressing thought, that he wasn't going to leave Samuel again.

Before anyone could say a word, though, Samuel and Jasper's phones went off in unison. "What time is it?" Samuel asked as if he was coming out of a trance, peering down at his phone. "Oh no. We have to get the Christmas Eve event set up! I knew I was forgetting something this morning."

"What does that entail?" Rory asked. "What needs to be done?"

"A ton," Samuel said, looking around. "Malcolm, Ty, you've done a ton so far, but—"

"Say no more," Ty said, already getting to his feet. "What do you need?"

"Gingerbread picked up from the bakery across town for the house-building contest," Samuel said, and he'd barely gotten the words out before Ty and Malcolm had disappeared. "Jas, you need to go pick up Grandpa so he can get ready to be Santa. He'll have that ridiculous sleigh with him, so it's good you brought a shuttle."

"What about me?" Rory asked, getting up from the booth to allow Jasper out.

"First, we're getting your shirt on the right way," Samuel said as Jasper left. "And second, you're going to tell me what you were too embarrassed to say in front of everyone else."

Chapter Twenty-Three

RORY PULLED his sweater off, turned it the right side out, and snuck a look at Samuel, who was sitting in the driver's seat of the parked truck on the phone with Juliet. God, he was beautiful. Genuinely beautiful, from the crow's feet that had appeared around his eyes in the last two decades to the faint scar on his upper lip from when he'd fallen off his skateboard as a kid, and while Rory had been somewhat uncertain about his proposal, he was now sure that this was where he wanted to be.

He looked away to avoid being caught, dragging his sweater back on over his head and therefore missing Samuel stealing a look at him as well. "Okay, Jules, thanks. Rory and I are stopping at the storage unit to pick up the rest of the stuff, but we should be back by one. You're a lifesaver, honestly. Thanks again." He hung up, looking over at Rory. "We have to get the pieces for the set we have for pictures with Santa."

"You guys really go all out, huh?" Rory asked, glad to avoid the elephant in the room for the time being. "What's the schedule for today?"

"This afternoon is the jingle bell bunny ski, which is just a little caroling thing Clark runs for the kids, but this evening we do pictures with Santa, a gingerbread-house-building competition, and top it off with a movie screening in the lobby," Samuel said, looking a little sheepish. "I know it's kind of over-the-top, but the families love it. We do good business at this time of year. Even some locals stay with us for the experience."

They sat in silence for a few moments before Rory managed to organize his thoughts. "I meant what I said at the cafe. I don't want to leave, Sam. When you kissed me the other night, I think it really made me…. I like New York, but I need to be here."

"You said that, but… I don't think I can afford to pay you what you're worth," Samuel said, eyes flitting toward Rory. "I mean, you're an award-winning architect. You shouldn't be trapped doing restoration for your…. Huh." He paused, flexing his fingers against the steering wheel.

"What 'huh'?" Rory asked, looking at Samuel.

"Well, I was going to call myself your ex-boyfriend, but is that still true?"

"Don't try to get me to define the relationship right now," Rory said, shaking his head. "Especially when I think you've misunderstood a huge part of this whole plan."

"What? What part did I misunderstand?"

"I'm not helping you restore the lodge because I think it's going to make me money or because it's some huge step forward in my career," Rory said. "I'm restoring the lodge because I want to be here with you, Sam. That's it. I have money saved up, and I can sell the condo for a place here and—"

"You should stay with me," Samuel said without hesitation. "No, not stay, that's not what I meant. You should live with me."

Rory, doing his best to pretend he hadn't hoped for that exact outcome, made a noncommittal noise. "I don't want to be an imposition, and Jasper probably doesn't want to have me hanging around."

Samuel snorted. "Are you kidding? I heard all about your heart-to-heart the other night. The kid has already accepted you as a second dad, whether you like it or not. Besides, as hard as he's trying to hide it from me before Christmas, I know he got early acceptance to NYU. He forgets that the mail doesn't magically appear in his room, and the envelope he got was way too heavy to be a rejection letter. I think he's worried I'll be a sad, lonely old man if he's not here, but all I've ever wanted is for him to be confident enough to do his own thing."

A sudden surge of affection overcame Rory, and he reached across the center console to pull on Samuel's wrist, lacing their fingers together as soon as Samuel relented and removed his hand from the wheel. "When we were kids, all I ever really dreamt about was being grown up enough to have a home with you. I think living together would be nice, even if we've had twenty years apart."

"I think so too," Samuel agreed, turning the truck into the parking lot of a storage yard. As much as they both wanted to talk more, to hash out the details, there was simply too much to do. Rory realized that he had been a snowball teetering at a mountain top, and being roped into helping with the lodge's Christmas Eve plans had been the last gust of wind to send him careening down the slope.

They had hardly finished loading the set pieces into the truck when Samuel's phone rang, Juliet on the other end. Clark had slipped and sprained his wrist during the ski event, and while he was fine, it meant he wouldn't be able to set up the portable movie screen for the evening's screening. It was another task on Samuel's plate that he clearly wasn't anticipating, and it meant that as soon as they returned to the lodge there was no time to be alone.

Rory offered to help but was quickly rebuffed, getting the sense that it would be more hassle to teach him than it would be for Samuel to do it himself. He headed up to his room, looking forward to a hot shower and the chance to think about what had transpired over the last day or so, only to find Malcolm and Ty sitting on Malcolm's bed, repacking Malcolm's suitcase and arguing. "What, uh, is going on? You guys can't have something to argue about already."

"Ty is leaving on the twenty-sixth, but you and I are leaving on the twenty-eighth," Malcolm said, folding a shirt with such precision that it was kind of scary. "I'm trying to get him to stay the extra two days, but he's not buying it."

"I have to get back to the city and put together the shots I took for the movie," Ty said, looking at Rory imploringly. "From my point of view, it makes more sense for him to come back with me. There's no more work that you guys need to do here, right? Your firm can't buy the place."

"He's got a point," Rory said, settling on his own bed to take his shoes off and looking at the pair. "Plus, I don't know if I'm going to head back on the twenty-eighth. The firm is closed for the holidays now, right? I'm gonna give them my notice after the New Year."

Malcolm looked down at the sweater he was holding in his lap. "I've never left a job early," he finally said, frowning. "And I've already made a huge sacrifice by helping you save the lodge. I don't want to risk my shot at making partner."

"I don't want you to worry about that," Rory said, looking at him. "I'm planning to take the blame entirely. I didn't tell anyone that we were coming to my hometown, I lied to you about my relationship, you get the point. Obviously this means that I went behind your back to have the lodge declared a historical landmark as well. I'm not sure how much they'll trust me after I tell them all this, but I plan on endorsing you for the partnership, regardless."

"It just doesn't seem real that you're quitting," Malcolm said, returning to folding his shirts. "Are you sure that this is the right thing for you?"

"I am," Rory said, surprised by his lack of hesitation. "I spent months going back and forth on whether I should leave for university and regretted the decision for months after. I know I'm supposed to be here with Samuel. Plus, getting the chance to restore an old building rather than designing a new one is exciting. I really think you should go with Ty, because I think that's where you're meant to be now too."

"See?" Ty asked, reaching out, gripping Malcolm's shoulder, and shaking him slightly. "You should be with me, okay? I think it'll be a good time."

A knock came at the door, and the three of them looked at each other, confused, before Rory realized it had to be for him. He got up and padded over to answer the door, and Louis Caldwell stepped inside. "What?" he asked in response to the look Rory shot him. "Jasper is too busy to tell me how it went this morning, so I came to ask you instead. Spill."

"Why am I suddenly the person every teenager in town wants to talk to?" Rory asked, but he let Louis in nonetheless. They spent the next few hours debriefing about what had taken place, Louis listening diligently and asking a litany of questions to nail down exactly what had happened. It was clear to Rory that the teen wasn't on his dad's side, that he was genuinely concerned about what would happen to the lodge, and that it seemed Jasper Daniels shared his father's ability to inspire total loyalty in his romantic partners.

The sun was beginning to set, and Louis was explaining the ins and outs of the program he wanted to take at NYU when the room phone rang. Rory answered it, Samuel on the other end. "The busy part is over," he said, sounding exhausted. "Juliet is running the gingerbread competition, so I've got a break before the movie. Do you want to come down here for dinner?"

"Sure," Rory said, Louis leaning in to listen, and Rory grinned. "Is Jasper free? Louis is pining."

"I'm not pining," Louis hissed, startled.

Samuel laughed at the same time, clearly amused by Louis's sudden protest. "He's taking a break, yeah."

"I'll be down in a few seconds, Sam." He hung up, got to his feet, and slid on his shoes. He and Louis took the elevator down together, parting at the bottom as soon as the doors opened, thanks to the sudden appearance of Jasper. It was clear he'd run over the moment his father had told him Louis was on his way down, but he at least had the manners to point Rory to where he'd last seen his dad.

Samuel was by the door to the kitchen, looking pleased but exhausted, and as Rory looked around the lobby, he saw Tim and Marion standing near a few low tables where families were assembling gingerbread houses. The Danielses were dressed as Mr. and Mrs. Claus and clearly judging the progress of the builders, and a flare of warmth struck Rory as he saw them, even before he was pulled into Samuel's arms and kissed on the jaw. "Finally," he said, his voice sending a shudder of delight through Rory. "We have approximately an hour before the contest is over. Come on."

He tugged Rory into the kitchen and over to the workbench, a set of plates laid out and loaded with food. "I asked the guys at the restaurant to whip up something good for dinner," Samuel said, pulling out a stool for Rory before settling into the one alongside him. "I thought it would be good to talk and eat."

"I want to make it so clear to you that I want to be here," Rory said, as earnest as he could possibly sound. "I know it's going to take a while for you to believe me, but I love you."

"It's not going to take a while," Samuel said. "I believe you. The noises you were making last night in the truck were enough to convince me."

"Okay, pervert," Rory said, blushing as he kicked Samuel's ankle lightly. "Do you really want me to live here with you? I can probably buy a house with the sale of the condo…."

"No, I want you here," Samuel said. "I can't be clearer than I already have been when I say I want you here, but I feel like I'm getting a lot more from this situation than you are. You saved my lodge, you're coming back…. What are you getting in return?"

"I'm getting you," Rory said, as though it was the most obvious thing in the world. "Sam, you have no idea how good it feels to have you. For years I thought I wasn't good enough, that there was some reason you hadn't come with me. To know now that it was just a string of bad luck is honestly enough." He grinned, knocking his foot against Samuel's leg again lightly. "And if you keep doing what you did last night, well…."

"Now who's the pervert?" Samuel asked, grinning at him.

Dinner was good, but the conversation was better, Rory making concrete plans to head back to the city and get his affairs in order before returning to Evergreen Hill, this time to stay. Rory was just beginning to outline the restoration he wanted to get completed first when the double doors to the kitchen opened with such force that one of them hit the wall. Both Samuel and Rory jumped, turning to see who it was, only to find Connor Caldwell standing there.

The change that had overcome him was honestly shocking, his face flushed and his hair disheveled. Gone was the composed and handsome man of the days prior, Connor brandishing a tablet at them as if it was a weapon. The moment after he entered, Louis and Jasper came in as well, Louis grabbing his father's arm. "Dad, you need to calm down," he was saying, but Connor shrugged Louis off and directed his attention to Samuel and Rory once more.

"Did you do this?" Connor asked, holding the tablet out as though it would explain what he was talking about. "I gave you a fair chance to sell me the lodge and you refused, I go through the proper legal channels, and you turn around and fuck me like this? You have no idea how easy it would be for me to ruin you."

Samuel began to get up, but it was Rory who got to his feet first, his dark eyes fixated on Connor. "Don't make me do this in front of your son, Connor," Rory said, Connor snapping his gaze to Rory in turn. "Do you know what my partner dug up on you while we were researching the injunction? A series of similar land filings, attempts across the country to strongarm properties based on nothing more than your desire and a hope that the owners don't stand up to you."

"Those were all legal—"

"Legal doesn't mean right," Rory shot back. "Was it right when you forced a care home to close in California last year? Or how about the charter school you had shut down in Brooklyn the year before that? Malcolm and I chatted with quite a few people who have very strong opinions on you."

Connor stepped closer, his face nearly purple with rage. "You're the reason he had the injunction blocked?" he asked, shaking the tablet at him as if it would explain things. "Who are you to do that?"

"Dad, come on," Louis said, something about his voice indicating he was no stranger to his dad's temper. "It's not worth it."

Connor shook him off again, this time more roughly than before, and Jasper stepped forward to pull Louis away in turn. "Who are you, huh? Some gay little architect meddling where he shouldn't? I could get you fired in a second!"

Rory couldn't help it, he laughed. He covered his mouth, so caught off guard by being called a gay little architect that he simply couldn't stop himself. The effect was immediate: Connor lunged at him, Samuel lurched forward out of his seat, and Jasper yanked Louis back out of the way, narrowly missing pulling the two of them into a pastry cart filled with danishes. Amid the chaos, there was still no mistaking the sound of the tablet in Connor's hand cracking against bone.

Chapter Twenty-Four

"I CAN'T BELIEVE he broke your nose with an iPad," Rory said, Samuel hissing softly as a cold compress was pressed to the bridge of his nose. "Why'd you launch yourself in between us like that?"

"He was going to punch you," Samuel said, sounding entirely stuffed up. He was sitting on the desk in the office, the lodge's first aid kit open beside him, and his shoulders were slumped like a kid who'd just been scolded. "I didn't even stop to think."

"Now it's gonna be all crooked," Rory said, lifting Samuel's hand to make him hold the compress in place. He unwrapped a butterfly bandage, looking over his shoulder. "Are you sure you didn't want an ambulance? What if you're concussed or something?"

"I don't want the cops showing up," Samuel said. He winced as he moved the compress away, doing his best to look pathetic. "I don't really want Louis's dad getting assault charges, even if he's an asshole."

"Lean down a bit," Rory said, carefully applying the bandage when Samuel did so. "Looks like this beats the mosh pit black eye but isn't quite as bad as the bicycle-oak-tree accident. I think you'll be hurting for a couple days."

"You shouldn't have hit him too," Samuel said. "You're lucky the boys intervened."

Rory sucked his teeth, placing another bandage on the other side of the cut before dabbing it with ointment. "I wasn't going to let it slide. If he was going to be so sensitive about being laughed at, he should've come up with a better insult."

"That didn't hurt your feelings at all? It hurt mine."

"Why?" Rory asked, scoffing. "I am a gay little architect. He didn't say anything wrong, he just said it as though it was a bad thing, and it's not." Samuel abruptly pulled him into a hug, squeezing him so tightly Rory was briefly breathless. "What?"

"I love you," Samuel said, and the words hit Rory right in the heart, his hands rising to grip the back of Samuel's shirt. "I mean it. I'd get hit in the face with an iPad every single day if it meant I could have you around."

"You have me around regardless," Rory murmured, kissing the side of Samuel's head. "I don't think getting hit in the head repeatedly is a good idea."

Samuel responded by squeezing Rory even more tightly, Rory laughing and hugging him tighter as well. They were interrupted by Clark pushing into the office. He'd been the one Jasper had fetched when it had seemed like the fight was going to escalate, and it was apparent that he was usually Samuel's backup when dealing with rowdy guests. "Oh, uh, am I interrupting?" he asked, turning back around with the tips of his ears turning red.

"Clark, come on," Samuel said, laughing. "What's up?"

"Connor is leaving, but he wants to talk to you," Clark said, turning around as Rory extricated himself from Samuel's grip. "Both of you."

"He's leaving?" Samuel asked. "What about his family?"

"His wife is packed and ready," Clark said, holding the door open and stepping into the hallway after them. "The kid says he's staying. He's eighteen, and the room is prepaid, so I guess it's technically fine, but it's pissed Connor off more."

"He's just having a tantrum because he didn't get the toy he wanted," Samuel said, clearly still irritated. "I told him I wouldn't kick him out as long as he didn't try to hit anyone again."

"I think his pride won't let him stay," Clark said. They fell silent as they reached the lobby, Tim and Jasper working on setting up a portable movie screen, although Jasper was shooting dark looks in the direction of the front desk. The Caldwells were standing there with Juliet, Cassie engaged in conversation with her, but both men were standing awkwardly, Louis watching Jasper and Connor staring stonily at the back wall. Rory was pretty pleased to see a purple bruise blossoming over the man's cheek from where he'd punched him in revenge for hitting Samuel.

As they approached, Connor turned to look at them, his fingers flexing on the handle of his suitcase. "Clark says you're leaving," Samuel said, some of his usual gruffness lost thanks to the nasal quality his nose was imparting. "You're welcome to stay until the new year like you were scheduled, as long as you stick to the rules I outlined before."

Connor frowned, his temper flaring, but a nudge from Cassie seemed to put him back on track. "I'm sorry I hit you, Samuel," he said stiffly. "And I'm sorry I insulted you, Rory. My wife has pointed out that since our boys are… friendly, it's in our best interest to keep things civil. We'll be leaving tonight, but I'll send the plane back for Louis in a week or so."

"He can go back to New York with me, if that works," Rory offered. Sending a private plane just to pick up one person rankled him. "I'm driving back on the second."

Connor eyed him before nodding once. "Fine," he said. "Work it out with him. As long as he comes back before his semester starts, I don't care."

"Thanks, Dad," Louis said, irritated. "I guess I'll see you then."

His mother hugged and kissed him, but Connor didn't move to say goodbye to his son, merely taking their luggage and leaving without another word. It was abundantly clear he wanted nothing more to do with the lodge now that he couldn't own it. Cassie said a hurried goodbye before following him, Louis watching his parents go before looking at Rory. "You'll actually drive me back?"

"Yeah, it'll be good to have the company," Rory said. "Malcolm is going back with Ty, so it was shaping up to be a lonely journey. Probably a little better for the environment too."

Louis peered at him, clearly assessing what to think before nodding. "All right," he said finally. "I'll take it. Sorry my dad tried to hit you." He grinned, suddenly mischievous. "He should be nicer to his future in-law." With that he jogged over to join Jasper and Tim, who were now setting up the seating for the makeshift theater.

"Are we getting married?" Rory asked, thoughtful.

"It sounds like he and Jasper are getting married," Juliet offered, looking at Samuel. "He really got you, didn't he?"

"Yes," Samuel said, groaning softly. "I haven't been hit in a while."

"It's like high school," Clark said, rolling his shoulders. He had just returned from walking the Caldwells to the door, clearly not trusting Connor to not try and burn the place down on the way. "You were always getting in fights for Rory." He paused, a smile flitting across his face. "I'm glad you figured it out, honestly. Me and Jules had a bet on if it would happen before or after Christmas."

"I owe him a date night now," Juliet said good-naturedly. "Thanks a lot."

With Connor gone and guests beginning to file in for the movie screening, Samuel rapidly became busy once again. Rory watched him for a bit, intrigued by the way he interacted with each and every guest as though they were of the utmost importance, but soon got distracted by the reappearance of Jasper and Louis. The kids' movie playing obviously wasn't very interesting for a pair of teenage boys, and they sucked Rory into a game of cards at the front desk that lasted for quite a while.

When the movie ended, Samuel made sure that the kids in attendance all saw him leave out milk and cookies for Santa before they dispersed. Taking down the screen and putting away the seats was all-hands-on-deck, but once that was done, there was nothing else to do. Clark and Juliet's kids, who had been in attendance for the day's festivities, were gathered up and left with their parents, Tim and Marion not far behind. After warning Jasper he needed to be back in their quarters by midnight—clearly remembering all too well what he'd gotten up to as a teenager—Samuel allowed him and Louis to hang out in Louis's room for the next few hours.

As quickly as they'd gotten busy, Rory and Samuel suddenly found themselves alone.

Samuel set up the front desk to indicate that he could be reached on-call and turned to look at Rory. "Do you want an early Christmas present?" he asked, Rory tilting his head to one side. "Come on."

"I don't think you should still be on your feet, Sam," Rory said, following him. "You've got a black eye now too."

"It won't take long, I promise," Samuel said, entering the kitchen and continuing through to the hallway that led to their quarters. "And then you can baby me all you want."

"What if I don't want to baby you?" Rory teased.

"Then I'll just make sad puppy dog eyes at you until you take pity on me," Samuel said, pushing into his quarters. Despite being a series of former servants' quarters that had been renovated into one area, the living space was actually quite open and airy, the walls covered with pictures of Samuel and Jasper, their family and friends. Rory was examining a picture of a toddler-aged Jasper looking like a marshmallow on the bunny slope when Samuel spoke. "Okay, don't look."

"I won't," Rory said, although the scuffling noises he heard from behind him were immediately intriguing enough that he thought about turning around. "Are you building it from scratch?"

"Shut up," Samuel said, continuing to do whatever it was he was doing. "I'm gonna grab your shoulders. Don't freak out. Oh, and close your eyes."

"So many directions," Rory said, but he closed his eyes nonetheless, Samuel's hands settling on his shoulders. He was carefully guided about ten feet away from where he was standing, Samuel letting go of his shoulders and taking hold of his waist. "Can I open them?"

"Hold on," Samuel said, and Rory could tell just from his voice that he was double-checking. "Okay, we're good."

Rory opened his eyes, finding himself facing an ancient brick fireplace. Three stockings hung from the mantle: a tartan one with Samuel's name embroidered on the cuff, a felt snowman that had all the hallmarks of having been made by Marion when Jasper was a baby, and a burgundy stocking covered in snowflakes that Rory recognized well. It had been his before he'd left, hung every Christmas alongside the Danielses' in their living room.

Nostalgia, adoration, and surprise struck Rory all at once, his eyes going wide at the sight of it. "Is that actually mine?"

"Yep, the original," Samuel said. "My mom found it when she was going through her Christmas stuff a few years ago, and I asked if I could keep it. I usually keep it in my room, but well, I have a reason to have it out now, don't I?"

Rory was quiet for a moment, his heart beating impossibly hard. "After I left, I stopped celebrating Christmas at all," he said finally. "I resented the people I saw spending time together, and even as I started to make friends, I felt like celebrating would make me miss you guys too much. It went from being my favorite time of year to the worst, just depressing and gray. That's part of the reason I wanted to come back here for work. I was hoping I could convince myself it had no effect anymore."

Samuel squeezed him, kissing him gently on the side of his head, and Rory sighed. "This entire time I thought I was growing, but I've just been running. I never stopped missing you or your family. I've loved you this entire time and haven't once realized it."

Abruptly, Samuel hauled him into his arms, peppering kisses along the side of his head and face. "You realize it now, don't you?"

Rory laughed, leaning into the kisses and gripping the back of Samuel's shirt. "Yes, yes! Now stop before you make your nose bleed again!"

"No," Samuel said, kissing his jaw. "No, I'm going to kiss you until morning unless you say you love me."

"Oh my God," Rory said, pretending to be annoyed. "I love you. Now your turn, got it?"

"I love you," Samuel said, dead serious. "And come morning your stocking will be filled, and you'll realize that every Christmas we've spent apart was just preparing us to be together again."

Rory looked up at him, Samuel's hazel eyes molten with unfettered adoration, and warmth flooded him from the inside out. "Merry Christmas, Sam."

Samuel grinned, leaning in more closely and stealing a kiss. "Merry Christmas, Rory," he murmured against Rory's lips, and Rory couldn't believe he'd ever thought himself unlucky in the least.

Epilogue

One Year Later

"A LITTLE TO the left," Rory said, tilting his head to one side as he peered up at the wreath. "I don't know, I kind of think it's crooked."

"It's a circle," Malcolm grumbled, but he tilted the wreath to one side nonetheless. "How did you rope me into this, anyway?"

"Consider it a deposit on your wedding venue," Rory said. "Ty volunteered you while he goes over the schedule for pictures with Santa."

Malcolm sucked his teeth but still did as he was told, straightening the wreath before clambering back down the ladder and facing Rory. Not much had changed in a year just by looking at Malcolm, the man still impeccably dressed and model-handsome, but the thin gold band on his left ring finger spoke to a fundamental difference. Between the engagement and making partner at the firm in the aftermath of Rory's controversial resignation, Malcolm was undoubtedly an entirely different person than he had been prior to last Christmas.

But then again, so was Rory.

The last year had felt like mere days, the restoration of the lodge a massive undertaking. Sourcing materials, hiring contractors, liaising with the historical society…. It all took time and patience, but with Christmas in just a few days, the vital restoration had been finished in time to meet the society's deadline. The future of the lodge was secure, and Rory had rapidly discovered that he was good at restoration, his eye for detail a huge boon. The society had already mentioned the possibility of Rory having more work in the New Year, but for the moment he was just reveling in the joy of the season.

"You know, when Ty brought up coming here for Christmas, I didn't think we would immediately be put to work," Malcolm said, dusting off the front of his sweater. "I thought we'd be relaxing, skiing, kissing in the snow, sitting naked in a jacuzzi…."

"Okay, that's more than enough," Rory said. "You're acting like I made you do hard labor, and not just hang some decorations. How did you become even more uptight in the last year?"

"Just for that, I'm not warning you," Malcolm said, raising one eyebrow before turning away.

Rory opened his mouth to ask what Malcolm was talking about when he was abruptly tackled, the force of the blow knocking him directly onto a nearby couch. Rory swore, caught entirely off guard, and wiggled around to find that the reason he had been hit with such force was because he'd been tackled by two people and not one.

"Hey, Dad," Jasper said, grinning down at Rory and pulling him into a sitting position. "Did we break your hip?"

"I'm not even forty yet, you brat," Rory said, looking between him and Louis. Jasper had really leaned into embracing the look of an artist, his hair grown into a shaggy mullet and his septum pierced, but Louis looked much the same, albeit happier than he'd been the Christmas prior. "How was the drive?"

"Jas sped the entire time," Louis said. "And he wouldn't stop playing this weird Christmas playlist."

"It wasn't weird. It's Dad's tree-decorating playlist, and it's guaranteed to get you in the Christmas mood."

Louis gave Rory a look that clearly said it hadn't put him in the mood before looking around. "Where is Samuel?"

"Uh," Rory said. "He was in the office with Ty, but I feel like Malcolm might have gone to warn them that you two had arrived."

"We saw them a couple weeks ago," Jasper said offhandedly, settling on the couch and hauling Louis into his lap. "They came to my first art show."

Rory smiled, deciding not to mention that he had texted Malcolm, asking him to go since he and Samuel hadn't been able to make it down to New York so soon after Thanksgiving. He was about to ask how the art show had gone when a pair of calloused hands settled on either side of his neck, and he tilted his head back before Samuel kissed him on the forehead. "Malcolm warned me there were intruders, but I didn't think it was this serious."

"Treating your own son like this, honestly," Jasper said. "What would Grandma say?"

"That you guys are just in time for getting lights on the big tree," Samuel said. "Did you really think you'd get away with abandoning your lifelong duty?"

"Ugh, what did I tell you?" Jasper said, resting his forehead against Louis's neck. "Not a second of peace."

"Let's go put our luggage away before you start crying," Louis said, hopping to his feet and pulling Jasper up after him. "Besides, I fell in love with you the day we strung the lights last year. That's a pretty good motivator, huh?"

"Sweet talker," Jasper said, kissing Louis briefly before taking his hand. "Sorry we broke your hip, Dad number two."

"I'm still not an old man, Jas, but you're forgiven," Rory said, groaning briefly in surprise as Samuel settled on the couch alongside him and hauled him against his side. Now alone, other than guests coming and going, Rory allowed himself to sink further against Samuel. "I'm glad they made it safely."

"Yeah?" Samuel murmured, his lips basically on Rory's ear. "I'm glad I have a couple minutes alone with you, baby."

Rory shuddered, looking over at Samuel and narrowing his eyes. "Why are you calling me baby?"

"I'm just happy," Samuel said. "Last year at this time I thought I'd lost you forever." He settled his forehead against Rory's shoulder, smiling. "And now we have a wedding to pull off in a week. No big deal, right?"

"We restored an entire lodge in a year," Rory said. "What's one measly wedding?"

Samuel laughed, lacing his fingers with Rory's. "I love you," he said. "I hope we never have another Christmas apart."

"We won't," Rory said. "I'm yours. I've always been yours."

Keep Reading for an Excerpt from
Ashford Hall
By Lee Ohlson

Part One—Summer, 1851

IT WAS by dint of my upbringing that I had spent scarcely any time beyond the limits of London at the age of twenty-eight, aside from the Eton schooling that a scholarship had paid for and the Cambridge education that had precipitated my career as a lawyer. The son of a retired English colonel and a woman from Karachi he had fallen in love with, I enjoyed a comfortable, but not lavish childhood, a middle-class existence that was nonetheless far less than I thought I deserved.

Having finished school nearly three years prior, I had been gainfully employed as a lawyer since. I had seen no reason to leave London, my cozy flat, my familiar haunts, for any considerable amount of time. A few days in France, a week or two in a country pile owned by some colleague or distant friend—neither of these constituted a true vacation from London, and as another sweltering summer approached, I found that for once I was struggling to imagine another three months hunched over the desk of my crowded law firm. It was barely June, and I could already taste the heat, feel the human crush of the city.

Most of the cases I had wouldn't go before a judge until August at the earliest, and the paperwork could all go where I went. There seemed little point in the years of work I'd done to become financially stable if I couldn't take some time away from the office to gallivant during the summer months, but as my desire to go away intensified, my uncertainty regarding where to go did the same. Leaving the country was my favorite choice, a little jaunt down to the continent within my grasp… and then the letter came.

For years after, I would wonder at the fact that the letter from Charles came at the same time my need to escape London turned into a full-blown obsession. My daily routine was the same—breakfast, work, a hansom cab home—but that day it had simply been too much. The heat was suffocating, the smell coming off the Thames stronger than usual, a shirt that had been comfortable when I'd left home now scratching the back of my neck where it met my skin. The thought of subjecting myself to this until the fall chill set in was unbearable, and by the time I returned home I was in a truly foul mood.

"A letter's come for you," was the first thing my landlady said as I stepped inside. She held a small cream-colored envelope in my direction. "It'll be that Ashford boy, I reckon."

A letter from Charles was a balm I hadn't known I'd needed. Charles and I had been friends since Eton, and our communication was both regular and lengthy, to the extent that the letter I held in my hand felt measly compared to the letters I'd grown accustomed to. However, Charles had an excellent habit of visiting me when he was in the city, and a short letter from him, perfectly timed at the beginning of June, was hopefully an indication that he cared to do just that. "Thank you," was the only thing I could say to avoid a deeper conversation, taking the letter from my landlady before running my thumb over my name written in the deep blue ink Charles favored.

I headed up to my flat on the top floor, a small and comfortable apartment that had once belonged to my landlady's son, and walked over to my desk under the window. The seal on the reverse of the envelope—a simple "C.A" in the same dark blue wax as his ink—came away easily against my ivory-handled letter opener and I was soon holding Charles's letter, written in a looping script I knew so well.

June 1, 1851
Dear Tom,
I hope this letter finds you well. I write from Ashford Hall, a place I am sure you are familiar with through numerous stories regarding my childhood home. I realized a few days ago that despite these years of friendship, I've never once thought to invite you here. I know your practice in London is busy, but the summer months are never pressing for the courts, and I am missing you terribly. My brother is a bore and a man can only ride his horse around the grounds so much before he tires of being alone.
If it isn't too much to ask, there is a room for you here, along with a balcony where you can work on your cases if you'd like. I think it would make both of our summers far more entertaining if we were to spend it together rather than

apart. I await your response, and if you decide to say no, just realize that I will spend the hottest months of the year in abject misery without my best friend.
Love,
Charlie

I could only smile, setting the letter down on the desk, leaning back in my chair, and looking out the window at London sprawling before me. At that time I was living in a fairly nice part of London, better than the neighborhood in which I grew up, but even there I felt innately smothered; as culturally vibrant as the city was, the idea of passing up the opportunity to spend a few months in the country, the air fresh and the company pleasant, was utterly unimaginable. I penned my response quickly in the spidery cursive that had served me well when taking copious notes in school but now meant I struggled to have my writing understood. I, of course, gave Charles a hasty yes, with the promise that I would be in Somerset no later than the following Monday after having the opportunity to tie up some loose ends in London.

Luckily, there was something about summer that made people amenable to requests they wouldn't have granted had they been made in the more oppressive winter months. By Friday at the end of work, myself and a carriage filled with various boxes were on our way to Somerset. The journey was, thankfully, not a particularly onerous one, although it was long compared to what could have been accomplished by train, and by the time the sun was setting over the country estate on Sunday evening, I was crossing the threshold into the esteemed Ashford Hall.

The stories Charles had told me over the years did not do the place justice in the slightest. As the estate was in the center of a massive forest, it took nearly half an hour to make it from the front gate posts to the inner walls, great stones meant to keep out whatever ancient enemies the Ashford family had stood against—although if I was being quite honest, I didn't believe there were any. The house was older than I could place, but there were more modern bits built onto it, including a cottage that sat at the edge of the woods for the deceased lord's former manservant and his family, the construction of which an undertaking I remembered hearing about my first year at Eton with Charles. Ivy sprawled up the stone facade of the house, including the roof of a large greenhouse attached to the manor that was currently reflecting the setting sun, and the sight of the manor home left me positively breathless. It brought to mind some great French palace, sprawling and beautiful, and for a few moments I was certain I had been brought to the wrong estate. I had never doubted that Charles had come from wealth, but this seemed an impossible home for a man like my friend to have been raised in.

The carriage driver stopped in front of the dual stone steps that led up to the home and before I could even dismount, Charles had thrown one of the great oak doors open and was hurrying down towards me. Knowing him, he had undoubtedly been hovering by the front door awaiting my arrival, and the idea that someone had been so eagerly anticipating me was enough to bring a lump to my throat, the loneliness of London having been endured for too long. I pushed the carriage door open, much to the chagrin of the driver, and stepped out onto solid ground for the first time since leaving the inn that morning. There was no time to recover from the rumbling of the road before Charles had me in a bone-crushing embrace.

It was rather like being smothered by an oversized blond dog. Charles had always been bigger than I was, my own good looks attributable to a slim build and dark, curly hair and no great robustness. Six feet and two inches, Charles was ash blond with wide green eyes and broad shoulders that had served him well when we'd been at school and other boys had been particularly mouthy about Charles's lack of a mother or my lack of a title. I'm embarrassed to admit that despite how ungentlemanly the hug was, I rapidly hugged him back, tangling my fingers in the fine fabric of his white shirt. It was nice to be greeted with so much excitement. This sort of affection was rare, my friends in London newer, posher, less prone to physicality like this, and I couldn't help but soak it in until Charles held me at arm's length. "You're far too thin, Tom."

"You saw me in April, you liar," I said, laughing as I finally removed myself from Charles's grasp. The carriage driver had already begun to unload the boxes, one of the stable boys assisting him in carrying them inside, and I realized for the first time that this was actually happening, that I was here for the summer. A true country estate, something out of an Austen novel, and it was mine to explore. "You're sure that this isn't an imposition?"

"Positive," Charles said. "Come along, I'll give you the grand tour and show you to your suite."

"Suite?" I asked, following Charles up the steps and pausing briefly to thank the carriage driver; I knew the man wouldn't expect it, but after traveling with someone for nearly three days, it felt like the correct thing to do. "I hardly need an entire suite."

"It's simply a bedroom and a sitting area with a desk. But you're on the same side of the house as I am, so we can bother each other as much as we please." He held the door open and I stepped inside; even in the summer heat the great hall was nice and cool, two large staircases mimicking the stairs out front and leading to each wing of the house. The great hall itself was lofty, the ceiling so high that it was difficult to make out the undeniably beautiful details that had been etched into place when the estate had been built centuries before.

Each subsequent room was just as stunning as the great hall; from the dining room to the ballroom to the parlor, everything was impeccably decorated and perfectly maintained. I do not mean to insinuate that I was raised in a home without means, for even retired my father boasted a fair salary, but our house had been small, and my mother had kept tenants, which made it feel even smaller. Compared to the wealth of Ashford Hall and the life I knew Charles had been raised in, my upbringing paled. I could see the ghosts of Ashford men wandering these halls, holding elaborate balls and hosting important members of parliament, and the history of the place captivated me from the first.

Finally, we came to rest on the eastern side of the house, a lavish hall decorated with art that seemed to have been plucked from master studios across Europe, and Charles indicated a beautifully carved door. "This is yours," Charles said before pointing down the hallway to another door on the opposite side. "And those are mine, so if you ever need anything, I'll be within shouting distance. Come along."

He pushed into the suites that would be mine for the summer, and despite his modesty at the front steps, I could tell that he was pleased with his choice for where I would be staying. I couldn't fault him as our lengthy friendship had ensured that Charles knew my tastes as well as I knew them myself. The room was light and airy, a balcony overlooking the massive gardens that lay to the east, a pond glimmering just beyond them. Clearly the maids had been working to air out the room, the linens freshly changed, the curtains pulled back, and the balcony doors flung open. "This is too much, Charles."

"That is simply not true," Charles said. "These rooms were where my mother hosted guests when she was still alive. I knew you'd be most comfortable here. The view was always her favorite, and you've always reminded me of her."

"Ah, your fondness for me is finally explained," I said, and he laughed, that bright clear sound that I had so loved as a boy. Charles was then, and had always been, the best of friends to me, and if I had known then the sort of peril that summer at Ashford Hall would put that friendship in, I would have turned heel and run back to London at that point. But I didn't, and the events of the summer did not, inevitably, tear us apart the way I once fathomed they would. Then, in that evening light, I believed that the secret I had kept from Charles since we had been boys was a secret that our friendship could not withstand.

"Even if you weren't like her, you would still be my friend," Charles said, leading me into a bathroom that led into the actual bedroom, set back away from the door so I would have some privacy. "Dinner is in an hour, time enough for you to freshen up. I've instructed Felix to bring your documents to your parlor here, but if I catch you going through them before the weekend is over, I will be quite disappointed. Remember, you've come here for pleasure as much as anything else."

"No law until at least tomorrow morning, I promise. I recall you mentioning a Felix you played with as a boy, but who is he now?"

"My brother's manservant, but he has temporarily taken over duties of head butler while our butler is visiting his daughter in Essex," Charles said. "You'll meet him soon enough. Don't be alarmed by his, uh, modern interpretation of his duties. As you know, Felix was raised alongside myself and Arthur and has always benefited from a rather elevated relationship with us compared to what you may have seen from other servants."

I smiled at this, shaking my head. "So you're warning me he has a penchant for argument? I am not so bothered by that as others in your stratosphere, Charlie. My profession means I frequently cross class lines."

"I know, I know. I just wanted to warn you. He offended one of Arthur's friends last time my brother had some lords down. You would have thought he'd called for the assassination of the queen, the way they reacted."

"Then Felix and I will get along quite well," I said. "I'll see you at dinner if I don't get lost on the way. And Charles, thank you. I can't imagine spending my time in London after seeing this place."

"You're always welcome," Charles said, pulling me into another brief one-armed hug before leaving me alone in the suite. As soon as the door snicked shut behind him, I wandered to the balcony, leaned against the railing, and peered out over the gardens. They were masterfully maintained, a sea of green with flowers and trees visible at intervals, and the fresh smell coming up off the plants was so refreshing I thought I could stay there for hours, simply breathing it in.

I was so taken by the scenery that I did not notice the man walking through the garden until he was nearly beneath my balcony, and when I finally spotted him, I found that I was looking at someone as exceptionally beautiful as Ashford Hall itself. He was tall, with broad shoulders and dressed in a perfectly tailored shirt and trousers, and I may have mistaken him for a well-dressed guest if not for his more than passing resemblance to Charles. While Charles was an open book, this man—Arthur Ashford, if my instincts were correct—had his brother's good looks with none of his easy charm. Rather, from my perch on the balcony, he seemed to hold himself with a haughtiness that was rather startling.

I had heard of Lord Ashford, of course, and Charles had always sung his praises. Arthur was said to be kind and effervescent, a sort of quasi-hero to Charles, who was three years younger and who had followed as closely in Arthur's footsteps as a second son could at that time. I had anticipated a copy of the younger Ashford, and to find myself now looking down at a man who could have been sculpted by Michaelangelo and easily landed among the most beautiful artwork known at the time was both unnerving and a fright.

Charles had never known the sort of man I was, the sort of man I *truly* was, the sort of attraction I had always harbored. There was a reason I was unmarried at my age, despite my profession and my looks, and it had nothing to do with a lack of interested women but everything to do with a lack of interest on my part. I had realized as a teenager that I had no use for women as anything more than friends, that men held for me the sort of beauty that I assumed I should have found in the fairer sex, and I had hidden this from Charles for good reason, unable to believe that my friend would accept this truth about me.

Seeing Charles's brother for the first time, I felt that untethered attraction rise like a snake coiling in the pit of my stomach. It was a moment of unguarded hunger and I paid for it dearly, because just as I became aware of my attraction, Arthur Ashford raised his head and met my eyes. He was terribly handsome, his face more hawk-like than his brother's, his eyes a piercing green framed by ash blond curls, everything about him screaming of pride. It was his expression, however, that sent fear lancing through me. Arthur studied me for the briefest of moments and seemed to read my mind, his lip curling in the slightest sneer before he turned away and continued on his walk.

I was discovered before I could even properly meet the man, and it was my own damnable fault.

Scan the QR Code Below to Order!

LEE OHLSON'S earliest literary memory is laying on her back in her bedroom listening to *The Hobbit* on audiotape while reading along in a mass market paperback to make sure she didn't miss a word. Early forays into fanfiction – self-inserts into *Lord of the Rings*, of course – and an ongoing collaboration with a middle school friend introduced her to writing for fun. After twenty-five years of ups and downs, including an entire 300-page manuscript lost to flooding during Hurricane Ike, she has finally reached a point where she can start working on publishing romance novels for a wider audience.

Lee Ohlson grew up in Houston, Texas, before returning to her home country of Canada in her early twenties. Outside of writing, she thrives on hiking, gardening, and swimming, as well as spending time with her two cats and two pugs. Her favorite holiday is Halloween, and she is an avid reader.

Some of her favorite books include *Pride and Prejudice*, *The Lord of the Rings*, *Lolita*, and *A Clockwork Orange*. Her favorite movies are *Fargo* and *The Thing*, and her favorite television show of all time is *Twin Peaks*. This eclectic mixture of media informs her works, and her adoration of different genres ensures that her novels are always fresh and compelling.

Lee's website can be found here: https://www.leeohlsenauthor.ca/

Follow me on BookBub

LEE OHLSEN

A SHADOW
COMES
DARKLY

Clark Wright's life as an ER nurse is turned upside down when he's attacked by a rogue vampire and left for dead. Saved by Alessio, a snarky vampire bartender with an unsettling connection to him, Clark is thrust into a dark paranormal world. As they hunt down Clark's attacker, they uncover a series of violent vampire killings plaguing the city.

Bound by fate and a magnetic attraction, Clark and Alessio must unravel the mystery while confronting their deepening bond and the strange dreams connecting Clark to his dead twin. Time is running out, and survival isn't the only thing at stake—so is their fated love.

Dark, erotic, and hauntingly seductive, this is a tale of fated love, betrayal, and the gritty underworld that hides beneath the surface of the city.

SCAN THE QR CODE
BELOW TO ORDER!

Fake it 'til you make it,
unless you hope to lose...

Convincing
Christmas

ELLE BROWNLEE

Jamie Crane, the ambitious young mayor of Hollingsford, Minnesota, is facing a holiday season like no other. His small town has been unexpectedly entered into a high-stakes reality TV Christmas competition, and with only days to prepare, Jamie must scramble to invent traditions out of thin air if he wants to keep Hollingsford in the running, which he isn't sure he does. As if that pressure wasn't enough, his first love, Jordan Miller—the boy-next-door turned successful lawyer—returns to town, stirring up memories of their secret teenage romance.

Once inseparable during the holidays, Jamie and Jordan have since gone in different directions—Jamie driven by his desire to improve his hometown and Jordan determined to leave his rough upbringing behind. But as they navigate the chaos of holiday events, old feelings resurface, and Jamie is faced with two dilemmas: keeping his town's dignity intact on national television and deciding if he and Jordan are meant to be together after all.

With a heartwarming mix of humor, nostalgia, and Christmas cheer, *Convincing Christmas* is a romantic tale of first loves, second chances, and discovering that sometimes, the best holiday traditions are the ones you create together.

SCAN THE QR CODE
BELOW TO ORDER!

STRUCK BY

Lightning

SARAH
BLACK

Marcus always thought life had a plan: paint by day, avoid commitment by night. But when he's literally struck by lightning in front of his apartment, things take a wild turn—especially when his cute, quirky neighbor, AJ, crashes his UPS truck after witnessing the whole thing.

AJ, a free-spirited dreamer with a big heart, heroically performs CPR to save Marcus's life. As they navigate the aftermath of the bizarre accident, their small neighborhood community rallies together. Tenesha, the outspoken single mom next door, along with her hilarious son Po and their mischievous dog Marco, become unlikely friends to both men.

While Marcus struggles to recover and AJ faces his own insecurities, the group leans on each other for support. As sparks of romance start flying between Marcus and AJ, the pair soon realize that fate might have more in store than either of them imagined.

When chaos threatens their lives again, AJ steps up, proving that lightning can strike twice—but love, once ignited, is there to stay.

Filled with humor, heart, and unexpected twists, *Struck by Lightning* is a feel-good rom-com about finding love when you least expect it and the beautiful messiness of community.

Scan the QR Code Below to Order!

COMFORT and JOY

NICKI BENNETT

It is a truth universally acknowledged that a widowed Earl must be in want of a wife—or so Marcus Stanthorpe's grandmother believes. Marcus had done what was necessary to ensure an heir, but now has no patience for his grandmother's matchmaking. Spending the holidays with his friends, his son, and his valet, William Haworth, brings him enough contentment.

But when a family emergency calls Haworth to London, Marcus's contentment reveals itself to be fickle. Suddenly he realizes how much William has come to mean to him. But William has never indicated he shares Marcus's preferences. Can the comforts of the holiday season bring two lonely men joy?

SCAN THE QR CODE
BELOW TO ORDER!

Money
can't buy
happiness.

SNOWED INN

MAYA BOYD

CEO Gordon Wyckoff lives for work and certainly has no interest in Christmas. When a blizzard runs him off the road, he ends up stranded in a picturesque mountain town that is the polar opposite of his fast-paced world. The Snowed Inn is the definition of the Christmas kitsch he hates.

Innkeeper Elliot Osterman can barely keep his quaint B&B afloat but has never been able to say no to a guest. One snowy night, he makes room for a stranded executive who knocks him out of his comfortable rut.

As the holidays take hold, the magic of the little town begins to restore their spark and unlock their hearts. Together these two mismatched men might be able to build a future, if they can just dig through all the history that's kept them frozen in place.

Scan the QR Code
Below to Order!

FOR **MORE** OF THE **BEST** **GAY** ROMANCE

DREAMSPINNER
PRESS

dreamspinnerpress.com

www.ingramcontent.com/pod-product-compliance
Lightning Source LLC
Chambersburg PA
CBHW071117100726
47908CB00008B/2399

* 9 7 8 1 6 4 1 0 8 8 8 0 0 *